The FIRING

The FIRING

Richard MacSween

Andersen Press • London

First published in 2002 by
Andersen Press Limited,
20 Vauxhall Bridge Road, London SW1V 2SA
www.andersenpress.co.uk

British Library Cataloguing in Publication Data available
ISBN 1 84270 055 3

*Extract from TO KILL A MOCKINGBIRD by Harper Lee published by Heinemann
by permission of The Random House Group Limited.*

Typeset by FiSH Books, London WC1
Printed and bound in Great Britain by the Guernsey Press Company Ltd.,
Guernsey, Channel Islands

For Jane, Alistair and George

1

There were two men at the front door. One of them was peering through the letter box, his backside pointed at Anna as she came up the path. Charming.

'Does Brian McManus live here?' the other one asked Anna.

They obviously thought they had more right to be on her front step than she did. They looked like they were from the council.

'Are you his daughter?' he asked, looking Anna up and down.

'No.' Sod you.

'Live here, do you? 7 Windermere Grove?'

'What's it to you?' she asked. 'Who are you anyway?'

He opened his mouth to reply, but she cut him off.

'Child molesters. I'm going to scream.'

The one who'd been peeking through the letter box had a go: 'We're looking for Brian McManus; there's been more complaints about this.'

He waved an arm at the road; 'this' was the pink Chevrolet parked there, if you could call something 'parked' that had no wheels and was on bricks. It had been like that since before Christmas. Brian's project.

'No, he's not my dad. But he does live here.' If Brian gets done by the council, that's his problem.

'Right, I see,' he said, keen to show how understanding he was.

'He's with my mum,' said Anna.

'OK. You mean, right now?'

'No, I mean all the time. Worst luck. But not right now; he'll be at work.'

His eyes narrowed a bit, clever.

'OK, so where's that then?'

'He's just moved jobs. I don't know where,' she lied.

'OK, we'll wait. Can we come in,' he hesitated, 'Miss?'

Yuk.

'I don't think so. He won't be back for hours. He'll go straight to the pub after work. He'll be back about midnight. In fact – ' she was starting to enjoy this ' – you can help get him into bed. He needs it when he's totally wrecked.'

They stared back at Anna.

'Right, we'll, er, we'll be writing.'

'Miss,' said Anna and smiled at him.

They clasped their folders to their chests, and went back down the path.

Anna unlocked the door and went into the house.

Brian was in the front room, peering round the curtains.

'What are you doing here?' she asked.

'I'm not so good today – must have ate something yesterday.'

'Oh yeah. Something you drank more like. Those men, it was you they were after, you know.'

'Somebody ratting on us again. I bet it was the

Phillipses. The woman's a born informer.'

The houses on Windermere Grove were once council houses but had been mostly bought up by their tenants. They'd had all sorts of fancy stuff done to them – porches built, lamps put up, and the gardens all planted and sorted. It was like a competition for smartest house. The Phillipses next door even had a pond with a fountain. Except it wasn't a fountain, it was a little stone boy taking a leak. Not what you'd expect to look at Mrs Phillips.

But Anna's house was still a council house, one of the very few left. It was grey concrete and had metal window frames with the paint coming off. One of the window panes in the front had got broken; Brian had sellotaped a black bin liner over it. It sucked in and out when the wind blew.

Nobody did the garden, not since they first moved in two years ago when Brian had starting digging it over 'to grow some vegetables'. He'd dug the bottom corner and then abandoned it – the bit he'd done was all bumpy and grass was growing over it. The spade was still stuck in the ground where he'd given up. And out in the street was the pink Chevrolet, on bricks. Everybody complained it made the street look untidy and now the council were giving them a hard time.

'It might not be her,' said Anna. '*Everyone* hates us.'

She went into the kitchen. There was a frozen pizza on the worktop, still in its wrapper, some oven chips in the wrong sort of dish, an opened tin of beans with the jagged top sticking up. The dribble of bean juice next to

3

it was the wrong colour. It was blood; he'd cut himself. He made an effort but it was all so pathetic.

'I'm off out,' she said.

'Your ma won't be long, Anna.'

'I'm off out anyway.' She wasn't going to be stuck with her mother's boyfriend, off work and hiding from the council, with blood all over the kitchen, thank you very much.

The twins were coming up the path. One of them grunted at her. She ignored them. She'd go and see if there was some action up at Sneck Cottage.

Sneck Cottage was right at the top of the village. Rachel was there, leaning against a wall, watching the building work being done on the cottage.

'Hi, Rach.'

Rachel scowled at her and turned back to watch as Glenn came running round the corner with a wheelbarrow full of rubble, up the plank and emptied it into the skip with a boom that sent up a cloud of gritty dust.

'Another pile of sh-sh-shine-a-light!' he announced from the end of the plank, grinning at them, suited that his audience had doubled, then disappeared round the back of the house again.

Rachel's dad was the builder. Glenn worked for him; he'd just left the school Anna and Rachel were at. They still had two years to do.

'Right, I've just found something out, about her that's bought the cottage,' said Rachel. 'She's got a son, like Glenn.'

'Like Glenn? You mean a retard?'

4

'I mean same age, smart arse.' She scowled again, what she thought was a withering look.

'Go on then,' said Anna. 'Tell us.' Rachel fairly took some winding up.

'I don't know nothing else, really. The mother makes pottery or something – that's why Dad's building this thing out the back.'

'Thing?'

'Yeah, for the pots and that.'

Anna thought Rachel a bit slow. In fact everybody in the village seemed a bit slow. Two years ago she'd been living in the city with her mother. On the backstreets of Manchester you could have a complete conversation – beginning, middle and punchline – in the time a typical villager got started. She looked longingly towards where she thought Manchester was, somewhere beyond Boltby, that hazy town in the distance. Boltby was where she went to school.

And new people were coming here; they must be mad!

'So tell us about this boy, then, Rach: name, height, hair colour, blood group.'

'I don't know. I haven't seen him.'

'I doubt they'll let him in the village.'

'Oh?'

'I mean, he might be a bit different. New people, new ideas. A bit dangerous that.'

'I just thought you might be interested, that's all,' Rachel sulked.

They didn't like each other, not really, but there was no one much else around, so you had to get on somehow.

Rachel was going out with Glenn. A year ago Anna had been going out with Glenn. It lasted a week. The high point had been kissing behind the village hall at the May Day Dance. They did it for hours, till Anna's jaw ached.

He came round the end of the cottage again, up the plank, and disappeared into the skip with the wheel-barrow, accidentally on purpose. He came up grinning in a cloud of dust. Rachel laughed herself silly, and didn't stop when he climbed out of the skip and began assaulting her; his arms round her, tickling and things, and Rachel squirming and squealing. They were always having these wrestling matches. Rachel's turn to get jaw-ache this May Day Dance, and it looked like Glenn was ready to go beyond kissing. Poor Rachel. Anna didn't want to hang around, it was just embarrassing.

She wandered round the back and peered through the window.

'What do you want, lass?'

Anna turned. It was Rachel's father standing in the door of the outhouse across the yard, a trowel in his hand.

'Only looking.'

'That's all right.' He softened a little. 'We've done in' house; we're on wi' this now.'

'What is it?'

'Come and have a look.'

Anna crossed the yard and went in. Not very exciting; a small room with stone walls, a concrete floor, a small window.

'What's it for?'

'It used to be a stable, from the look o' stuff what were in it. But she – ' And Glenn's father rolled his eyes and put on what he thought was a posh accent: 'She is having it for her kiln.'

'Oh, yeah; we've got one at school.'

There were wooden steps in the corner, going up. Anna walked over to them.

'Aye, there's an upstairs an' all; go on, have a look.'

And Anna hesitantly climbed the stairs, and was immediately in a very different room. Where downstairs had been cold, this was warm; instead of concrete there was a wooden floor, fragrant, pale gold in the sun that shone though the small window. The ceiling sloped down, following the roof. It was so low at the sides you had to stoop. It was brilliant.

'Why's a stable got an upstairs?' she shouted down.

His head appeared, level with the floor.

'It were a pigeon loft. You could tell, from t' mess. Anyroad, I've got to get on, lass. Go and see if you can persuade our Rachel to leave Glenn alone, so as he can get some work done.'

Anna reluctantly climbed down the stairs. If that's what builders did, weren't they lucky?

2

'Your da's been on the phone, Anna,' said Brian when they got back. No one else called her dad that; it was just Brian pretending to be more Irish. Ma and Da. 'He said he'd ring back later.'

'Great! When, did he say?'

'Oh, just later.'

'Did he say when I could go over?'

'I think he mentioned it.'

But when Anna played back the ansaphone, which had Brian's voice on it too because he was too stupid to know how to work it, there had been no mention of Anna going over to see her dad.

'Hi, it's your dad, Anna, and I was just ringing to say, by the way it's Wednesday teatime, I was – '

'Hello, Mick, it's Brian. How's it going?'

'Oh, hi, Brian. What're you doing home?'

'You know how it is, mate, once in a while you've got to break out!'

'You're right. All work and no play – '

'I think this machine's still on. D'you know how to stop them?'

'God knows. Isn't there a panic button?'

'Could be; I'll try this.'

There was a screech out of the machine. Anna looked

at Brian who shrugged and grinned. But the message went on.

'Jesus, Brian, what was that? That machine needs attention.'

'Not the only one, Mick, this human machine needs looking at too –'

'Hey, that's dead interesting, mate, but look, I need to get on. Is Cath there?'

There was another screech and that was it.

'Gripping stuff,' said Anna. 'So did I get a mention?'

'Oh aye, there was more but it's not recorded.'

'And he's ringing back?'

'He said so. Definite.'

'Who was definite; you or him? You're pathetic!'

'If you hadn't cleared off when you did, stayed to help with the tea, you could have spoke to him yourself. What d'you think I am – your bloody personal assistant?'

'Why didn't you just leave the ansaphone to get the message? Or else find out how it works? I mean, listen to the two of you!'

'Hey, calm down, you two!' said Anna's mother, coming into the hall.

Anna ignored her.

'He'd sooner talk to my dad than talk to me!'

'Anna!' warned her mother.

'Oh, forget it!' And Anna slammed out of the room.

It was mean, playing the emotionally disturbed daughter card yet again, but it never failed. They couldn't get you for it.

Her dad was still in Manchester – and he hadn't got a phone. He'd stayed there when Anna and her mother came over to Whin to live with Brian and the twins. Anna hoped it wouldn't last. The thought of her and her mother loading their bits back into a van – it'd only need to be a small van – and going away from this horrible, small village, all sky and sheep, was the only thing that stopped her going mad.

And they'd be going back to her daft, smiling dad in Manchester. Please.

The twins had taken their tea to eat off their knees while they watched telly so that left the three of them at the kitchen table. After taking the day off work, Brian was trying hard to get into Anna's mum's good books. For him trying hard just meant making conversation.

'Guess what, Cath; Whin's just got its first Ms.'

'First what?' said Anna's mum.

'Mizz or muzz, however you say it.'

'He means a woman who doesn't want to be a Mrs. Can't imagine why,' added Anna sarcastically.

'Right. She's not married and she's *not* not married. So what is she?' asked Brian. He waved his fork with a thumb that had some bloodstained tissue wrapped round it.

'What's it matter?' said Anna's mum. 'Who cares?'

'But if it doesn't matter, why do it?'

'If it doesn't matter, why not?'

'Because . . . ' said Brian, run out of argument: 'Well, why?'

He'd come back from talking to his mates, annoyed about something, and then, without trying to, Anna's mother made him look silly. Which made him angrier and Anna's mother feel guilty, so she tried to get him off the hook. Which made Anna mad. She'd have just let him dangle; it was his own fault.

'Anyway,' said Anna, 'you're not married.' She instantly regretted it in case it gave them ideas.

'I'm still married to the twins' mother, as it happens.'

'Oh, very meaningful, I'm sure!' said Anna.

'Anyway, Brian, who is she, this Ms?' asked Anna's mother.

'Her that's moving into Sneck Cottage, Jimmy Tat was telling us. She's not in yet but she's had some post.'

Jimmy Tat was the village postman. He had X-ray eyes. He knew what was in envelopes and parcels, better than the people who got them did. He knew which losers wrote to the Prime Minister, who was late paying their bills, and who only got junk mail. And because he was up and about early he also knew who hadn't been home all night, who was up early, and who was off sick when they should have been at school or at work. He knew everything. And he passed it on every night to whoever was listening in the village pub. That meant Brian brought it home pretty quick.

'Ms – wait for it – Colette St John,' he said, stressing each word. 'Moving in next week, with her son. Nobody knows about any father.'

That's how pathetic it was; a woman with an unusual name and her son move into the village, just two new people, and it's big news. And what was really pathetic was Anna had got so Whin-ified even *she* thought it was a major event. God, get her out of here!

'Anyroad, Jimmy Tat says he's onto the case. Jimmy'll find out what's what. Ms Colette St John!' he repeated and laughed.

'It's different,' said Anna's mother. 'A bit of class. Something like that would be right for the salon, don't you think, Anna? *Colette's*.' The hairdressing salon was her mother's grand plan. Just now she worked from home; so Anna and the twins had to behave themselves or clear out when she had customers in.

'I like those puns,' said Brian. 'You know, *Curl Up and Dye* – spelt dee wy ee – that sort of thing.'

'That's sad,' said Anna. 'They're just so out of date. There's like only four jokes you can make about hair and everybody's heard them a million times.'

'Ah well, the ladies know best,' said Brian standing up. 'Sorry I can't wash up, Loyalist bastards got me thumb.' He waved his tissue-wrapped thumb at them. That was one of his things; he was an Irish freedom fighter and the Protestants were out to get him, if Anna understood it correctly. It was just stupid.

'I'm off outside, working on the car. I'm fed up of having the council on my back.' He hadn't said they'd been round today and he'd hidden behind the curtains. 'And if I find out who's been grassing me up, I'll kill them.'

Anna stayed in all night, and got some tedious homework done, but her dad didn't ring back.

12

3

The woman was right over her before Anna knew it.

Anna was coming round the corner, looking at her feet and thinking it was time she stopped wearing trainers, when she heard footsteps.

Looking up, she saw the woman striding down the hill and only a few feet away from Anna. She was thin as a knife, even though she had on these baggy trousers and baggy top, all a sort of dull blue colour, and she had her hair up in a tight knot. She stepped into the road to avoid Anna, but gave her a sharp smile at the same time. The van that was going past hooted at her. She kept going down the hill, leaving a weird scent behind her.

Anna stood and stared after her. That could only be Colette St John.

That morning Rachel had told her on the school bus, 'They've moved in.'

'Who?' Though Anna knew of course.

'Sneck Cottage. Yesterday. And the son's called Wolf.'

'What kind of name's that?'

'Pretty dumb, isn't it?'

'How d'you know?'

'Me dad said. Something German or something.'

'Not the hairs growing on the back of his hands, then?'

'Eh?'

'Never mind. I'll come up tonight; we'll check him out, eh, Rach?'

But now Anna had already seen the mother before she'd even got up to Sneck Cottage.

Outside the cottage one of those hunchbacked French cars was parked up, brilliant yellow, with the roof rolled back. Rachel was already there, backed against the wall by Glenn who was interfering with her and saying, 'Had enough? Had enough?', all of which had her in helpless tears of hysteria.

'Hi, guys,' said Anna. 'Love-making skills coming along nicely I see, Glenn.'

Rachel scowled at her. 'So what would you know about it, Miss Frigid?'

Anna ignored this.

'Has the wolf-boy been spotted? Chasing sheep on all fours? Howling at the full moon?' she asked.

'No one's seen him, yet, but you should see the mother, Toilet de Whatever-she-is.' Rachel and Glenn spluttered at each other. 'She's wearing this – '

'Yeah, I saw her down the village. She looked great, didn't she?'

'If you like that sort of thing,' said Rachel.

'I'll tell you what, Rachel. Whin village needs all the help it can get.'

Glenn watched them, his mouth hanging open. Well, it wasn't but it might as well have been.

'If you think it's so lousy here, why don't you clear out, back to where you came from?' said Rachel. 'If it's so much better. If we're all too thick for you.'

'I'm not saying that. It's just if there's anything different happening you don't know how to handle it. It must be bad, get rid of it. In Manchester – '

'See what I mean?' said Rachel, turning to Glenn for confirmation. 'Manchester; the only place where anything ever happens! Well, why don't you – '

'Nice of you to give my home an inaugural row!' said a new voice behind Anna. It was the woman.

She wasn't out of breath though she must have walked from the shop – if that's where she'd been and there was nowhere else – and back up the hill in a nanosecond.

'Do you live in Whin?' She said it funny, a new word for her. 'I've met Glenn before, and Ruth just now.'

'Rachel,' Rachel corrected her and scowled.

'Sorry – let me off this once, will you? And who are you, if I might ask?' asked the woman.

'Anna.'

'Anna. That's a palindrome.'

'You what?' said Rachel.

'The same backwards as forwards. Anna, Anna. Get it?' She used her finger to show the word going each way.

Oh my God! Who is this?

'I'm Colette,' and she held out her hand.

Anna had no choice but to shake it. She hoped she did it right. The woman's hand was cool and slender. She saw Colette's top had a wavy line sewn into it in a darker shade of blue, like the sea in the evening. It wasn't Next, or even Monsoon; it certainly wasn't Marks & Spencer. It made her shiver looking at it.

'What about Nan?' said Anna.

'Yes, that's another,' said Colette.

'Though it's not really my nan's name – just what we call her. Her proper name's Margaret. Backwards that'd be Tragram or something.'

Colette laughed. She reminded Anna of one of those teachers who work too hard to make you like them, all isn't-this-interesting and aren't-we-very-equal. Except it was interesting, and Anna needed something.

Glenn and Rachel glanced at each other and said nothing.

'Fancy a drink, if I can find the teapot?'

She brought them all some funny-tasting tea in mugs with an odd mother-of-pearl glaze. They tipped it over the wall when she wasn't looking.

But in all the time they were there, there was no sign of the Wolf, even if the sheep were bleating on the other side of the wall.

4

Declan and Diarmid were being completely unco-operative. Anna's mother had asked her to get them to tidy up upstairs and they wouldn't; they just ignored her, smirking at each other. Their floor was covered with computer game boxes, dead underpants, empty Coke tins, an old sandwich. You didn't even want to walk across it, you didn't know what you might put your foot in, so she just leant round the door and yelled at them. They just smirked back at her from the computer – surfing the net, exterminating aliens or whatever ten-year-old boys did. Brian couldn't sort out a car that actually went but the twins could go on the internet if they pestered long enough. And that meant anybody trying to phone couldn't get through when they were using it. Like her dad. Probably.

Her mother came to the foot of the stairs and told her to stop shouting. She had a customer downstairs and they didn't want to hear her ranting and raving, so just tidy up quietly.

Except it wasn't her turn and *her* room was OK – it was everywhere else that was a tip. On the landing there was a skateboard, some pairs of dirty trainers, a video machine that didn't work but Brian wouldn't throw out.

The bathroom was disgusting. There were soggy

towels on the floor and a grey smudge round the inside of the bath. The soap was lying in a pool of gloop in the dish and the flannel had the slimies. The bog had two black pubic hairs stuck to the side, not hers or her mother's. It all stank of whatever it was Brian squirted on himself, which didn't quite cover up the smell of where the twins missed the bog.

No way was she doing it.

She went downstairs and straight out of the front door, pretending not to hear her mother calling her. Brian was working on the car. He was right underneath it with his legs sticking out, singing his Chevrolet song. It meant he was happy, when he sang. He'd started with that song when he got the car. It was some ancient American song that had a chorus that went:

We're on our way in the Chevrolet.
Goodbye to being a loner.
Every day in the Chevrolet
We're going to hit that homer.

But when the twins asked him what a 'homer' was, he didn't know. Maybe something to do with baseball. That was Brian for you: half a story and a job half done.

'Hiya, kid!'

He'd spotted her feet, and came out, twisting his head round with one eye closed so dirt didn't fall in it.

'Where're you off?' Brian asked.

'Ooh, let me see. Tonight's range of exciting alternatives. I could go and have a stimulating chat with Mrs Townson while I buy a sherbet dip, count the cows in the bottom field and see if I get the same as yesterday...'

'OK, kid.'

'...queue for the Workingmen's Club so when I'm old enough to get in and they start letting women in, I'll be just about dying of excitement.'

'They let women in now, on Saturdays.'

'Thank you, Brian. You're so understanding.'

'I didn't mean...I'm sorry there's bugger all to do. Isn't there anything on the telly?'

'Mum's doing a customer.'

'She doesn't mind the telly on.'

'It's crap anyway.'

'Nobody playing out?'

'*Playing out*? How old d'you think I am?'

'Anyway, kid, we'll soon have wheels. A few days and this – ' he patted the Chevrolet like a farmer patting his cow '– this will be ready for the road.'

Anna now saw that it had its wheels back on; so that's why the hallway wasn't as cluttered.

'I'll believe it when I see it,' she said, but it still gave her a little flicker of hope.

'And all the council spies,' he raised his voice so the street could hear it. 'All the bastard council snoops can take a running jump!'

'Yeah, OK, Brian. Fix it first, then you can start shouting the odds.' Anna walked off down the road. God, what was he like!

Colette St John came to the door immediately.

'Bob,' said Anna.

'Sorry?'

'Bob. It's another of those palindrome girls' names.'

'*Girls'* names?'

'There's a girl at school called Bobby. Sometimes we call her Bob.'

'All right, I'll give you that one.'

Pause. She was in green today, bluey green.

'And that's it, for now,' said Anna.

'It's more than I've come up with. D'you want to come in?'

Why not? In fact, yes. Yes.

After the sun it was cool and dark inside, so dark Anna couldn't see anything for a moment. There was a table in the middle of the room, a kitchen she could now see it was, with a vase of some sort of deep red flowers on it. A book open, face down. A hardback book. And nothing else. No ketchup, no set of spanners, no styling mousse, no football shorts.

'I've just about got everything out of boxes, you know how it is – well, perhaps you don't yet, but you'll find when you move house – '

'Why did you come here?' asked Anna.

'Oh, various reasons.'

'It's OK if you don't want to tell me.'

'It's complicated, but let's say things were getting a bit heavy where I was.'

Anna nodded, but felt something was being kept from her. Because she was only a kid? Or because the woman wasn't telling anyone?

'Anyway, you're not from here, are you, Anna?'

'How d'you know?'

'Oh, I can tell. The way you look at your friends.'

20

'What? Glenn and Rachel? Friends?'

'Exactly. You despise them but they're doing their best. They didn't choose to be here either.'

'They're from here. And never want to leave. Glenn wants to be a builder and Rachel wants to have babies with him, and he'll spend his nights round in the Workingmen's Club and she'll stay in and watch "Friends". And the babies'll grow up and do the same. Aaaagh!'

'You never know, they might be happy, even if it wouldn't do for me. Or you. Do you want something to drink?'

'OK.'

'Tea?'

'OK.'

'Promise me one thing; you won't tip it away when you think I'm not looking.'

Anna opened her mouth to deny it – and realised she'd be wasting her time.

'But it tasted weird.'

'It's got some China mixed in, China tea. Try it.'

And this time when Colette St John handed Anna the mother-of-pearl mug with the peculiar tea, she sipped it as though it were membership of a new club.

5

It was her dad on the phone.

'*Is that you, Anna?*'

'Dad!'

'*How you doing, pet?*'

'How'm I doing? I'm living in Whin, didn't you know? It was a one-horse town till the horse died of boredom – and you ask how I'm doing?'

'*Well, apart from that.*'

'There isn't anything apart from that – that's what I do all the time.'

'*School OK?*'

'School OK? You're going to be asking me what I had for my tea next. School's school, isn't it. Next question.'

'*You haven't lost your edge, have you, angel, living there? Perhaps it's doing you good.*'

'Any more cracks like that and I'll divorce you. When are you coming to take me away from here? And Mum too.'

'*She said it was fine, last time we spoke.*'

'She said, she said. If you want my opinion – '

'*I know you'll give it to me anyway, pet.*'

'Too right. Mum would kill to be out of here. And that's fine by me, provided it's Brian she kills or one, preferably both, of the twins.'

'*Declan and – what's the other one called?*'

'Diarmid. Irish mythical heroes or something – you know what Brian's like. Myth; ha! They get up, eat their mythical breakfast, grunt, go to school, come home and have tea, grunt, play on the mythical computer, go to bed. Grunt in their sleep. Very mythical.'

'*You're taking the myth.*'

'Oh Dad, it's not funny. Can't we, I don't know, do something else?'

'*Look, pet, point number one, your mother and me are no longer an item, as they say –* '

'Yes, I had noticed.'

'*In which case we're not going to live in the same house. And point number two, the flat I am living in is rented and there isn't room for you.*'

'Oh, thanks.'

'*I mean, there's room for you to kip when you come over – I'll sleep on the settee – but for now there's no space. Sorry, pet.*'

'Yeah. So when's that going to happen?'

'*What?*'

'Me coming over to visit?'

'*Any time you want. Soon as you want.*'

'When?'

'*I'll fix something up in the next week or two. Can you put your mother on the phone?*'

'All right.'

'*Sorry, pet, any other news?*'

'Other? I haven't told you any. But yes, new people in the village – they must have done something terrible to

23

be sent here. Or person, **there's** meant to be a son but no one's seen him yet. So **perhaps** he's another of those myths. Colette's OK. **Quite interesting**, really.'

'*Who?*'

'Colette, the mother. If there's a son. Brian made this big performance out of her being a Ms.'

'So she's not a myth.'

'God, Dad, I miss your pathetic jokes! She does pottery, she's got a kiln and everything up there.'

'*Very arty-farty.*'

'I don't think so, I mean she does it for real, to make a living. She's nice.'

'*So there is someone worth talking to in Whin. Things are looking up. Look I've got to go, can I have a quick word with your mother?*'

'I'll get her. And fix up me coming over there. Soon.'

'*OK, pet. Say howdy to Brian and the Druids from me.*'

'No. 'Bye, Dad.'

6

It was so quick and like nothing Anna had ever seen before. The wheel and the clay on it was a spinning blur, and Colette took hold of it and something magical happened; a form, a pillar of this shining chocolate-red clay rose between her wet hands. Then she pushed a thumb into it and it spread out so you could see how it would become a bowl.

'Wow!' She would have been embarrassed to have heard herself, how impressed she was.

Colette smiled.

'Good, isn't it? I still get a buzz from the clay taking shape in my hands. The trouble is, there's bills to pay so I have to do mass production instead of designing them the way I want to. Turn them out as quickly as I can, sell them, make some more, so it spoils the pleasure a bit.'

Anna just watched and let her talk.

'Load the car up, take them to some fair somewhere, set them out, and then watch people pick them, say how nice they are – and put them down again when they see how much I have to charge.'

Colette's hands reminded Anna of her mother's hands when she was doing people's hair. They had a life of their own, moving in a little dance, with absolute precision, using things like scissors or a spatula as

25

additional fingers, and all of this going on while their owners talked and laughed and looked round. Their hands were like people in their own right, two friends working together.

'Can I have a go?'

Colette laughed. 'It's harder than it looks. I wouldn't start with throwing.'

'Throwing?'

'What I'm doing. It's called throwing.'

'Why's it called that?'

'I don't know. I suppose the way you have to throw the lump of clay onto the wheel, to make it stick properly.'

'So throwing's making them as well as smashing them up?'

'I suppose you're right.' She laughed again, then asked: 'A lot of pots get smashed in your house, then?'

'Don't ask. Put it this way: we could keep you in business full time.' But Anna knew it wasn't true really.

It was the first time she'd been in Colette's studio, the first time she'd been in anything anyone had called a 'studio'. After the warm spring sun this had a nice cool mud smell, and with the splash of water round the wheel, well, you could see what hippos got out of it.

Colette lifted the finished bowl off, and then started another, thumping the clay onto the wheel. Her hands ran with a red slick, and as the shining dome of clay appeared between them, Anna said: 'It's like a baby being born, all that blood and this thing coming out.'

'Oh yes? And how would you know, Anna?'

'You know, TV and that.'

'I think most women would think making pots is easier than having babies. Children.'

So, tell us about Wolf, Colette.

'Have you got any children?'

Colette paused momentarily, then said, 'Yes. I've got a son. He's coming here soon. You'll meet him.'

'Does he live with his dad?' asked Anna.

'Anna; you'll meet him soon enough.'

Colette obviously didn't want to say any more; fair enough. But for a moment Anna had a glimpse of a more defensive person, not the very sorted woman who strode through the village in amazing clothes and knew her own mind.

Only for a second.

'But if you insist on throwing a pot, well, so you shall.'

'Cool!'

And ten minutes later Anna found herself sitting at the wheel, holding this silky tower of clay. Easy! But then it started to wobble slightly, and then waggled like a belly dancer on E, and she screamed at Colette to switch off the wheel before it got thrown into orbit.

'Don't worry, you'll soon learn. You've got a feel for it, I can see. Here, we'll start with a thumb pot so you can get used to the clay.'

'Thumb pot! We did those at primary school.' But she got down to it all the same.

Later Colette showed her the kiln in the outhouse, and the racks of pots and bowls; some waiting to be fired, others already 'biscuit fired'. Colette explained that clay was just mud; firing it in a kiln was what turned it into a sort of stone. That made Anna think the kiln itself was an oven where strange cooking, strange transformations went on.

Thank God there were still some new things waiting to be discovered; she'd resigned herself to dying of boredom.

7

Well, hello, Cath and Brian and Anna and Declan and Diarmid, and I'm sorry you're not available to take my call right now, but don't you think you could find a few more names to go on your message, there must be the odd goldfish or gerbil you've missed – hi, Anna, sorry I haven't been in touch for a while, what with one thing and another – oh, it's Monday, by the way, early evening, who cares – but the news is, Saturday week I'm borrowing a mate's motor and coming over to see you, take you out somewhere, Anna, if that's OK, Cath, and Brian and – er – the Donnelly twins or whatever the hell you're called – sorry, 'scuse language – that'd be Saturday the – er – 16th of, no the week before so that makes it the –

Screech.

Yes, Dad, yes.

8

There were two big events in Whin's year: the May Day Dance, and Bonfire Night. People from Whin talked about them as if the entire planet knew about them and cared about whether they were a success or not.

The May Day Dance had finally come round again.

Anna had been to last year's; she knew what to expect. It was held in the village hall where there were car boot sales at weekends, aerobics classes one night, line dancing had just started on another night. Thursdays was the youth club: ping pong, Coke and crisps. Like the others, Anna only went because there was nothing else to do.

Tonight there were flashing lights and a bar had been rigged up at the far end. Most of the men and some of the boys were drinking themselves silly. Earlier there had been an Irish fiddler, a friend of a friend of Brian's, who'd been a complete disaster of course. Now Mr Greenhalgh, who reckoned he'd once been a DJ, was playing these ancient records.

The little fantasy Anna had allowed herself this year was to imagine her dad would turn up, and dance the legs off everyone else. He was a brilliant dancer. Staring across the empty dance floor she imagined it full of dancers. Two by two they would give up and sit down, exhausted and put to shame by her mum and dad. They would be the only two still dancing as midnight struck. Then they would run out of the village hall and jump into the horse-drawn coach, pausing just long enough for Anna to jump up with them before rattling off into the night away from Whin and all the –

'Want another drink, kid?'

Brian paused in front of her, smiling and swaying slightly. He was off his face.

'Nah.'

'Go on, spoil yourself. 'T's on me.'

'God! Just leave me alone.'

Brian looked hurt, puzzled and happy all at the same time. Anna couldn't stand it. She got up and moved to another empty table. Brian stood for a while, then meandered over to the bar.

What everybody went on about was how Whin's May Day Dance was for families, to be together, it didn't matter how young or old. But just look at it! Mrs Thingy's new baby asleep; that little Chloë Strickland way past her bedtime and screaming her head off; Declan and Diarmid and their friends outside the door, sneaking cider; Rachel and Andrea in and out all night, having little dramas about who's with who and who's snogging who. Then there's a bit of an age gap because any girl who's hit sixteen wouldn't be seen dead here and would be out in Boltby or Manchester. Glenn and his mates haven't worked out how to get out of Whin yet so they're here, drinking. The only ones who are really enjoying it are the mums who are having the odd dance – with each other of course, because the men are too busy drinking and are pathetic dancers anyway. Marooned round the edge of the room are the oldsters, and they looked ready to go before it started. Welcome to family life in Whin; welcome to the May Day Dance. Well, thank God she wasn't in a proper family.

Her mother came and sat down.

'You've upset Brian.' She tried to sound casual but Anna could tell she was upset.

'He noticed, did he?'

'He said he only tried to get you a drink. And you bit his head off.'

'If only!' But the thought! Biting Brian's head off! Yuk.

'I wish you wouldn't get at him all the time, Anna. He tries his best with you.'

'Yes, well, he'll have to try a bit harder.'

Rachel came across, probably with some tedious will-you-go-out-with-so-and-so type message. 'It's him!'

'Sorry?'

'Look!'

And into the room walked Colette, wearing tight, well-cut jeans and a cream linen jacket. All the middle-aged eyes of Frumpsville turned to stare. Behind her was this small dark boy in black who obviously didn't want to be here.

'Must be the Wolf!' hissed Rachel. 'How old would you say?'

'Thirteen-ish? Too young for you, Rachel.'

'I'm not looking. I've got Glenn.'

'Oh yeah. Lucky you. Ah well, Rach, big build-up, big let-down.'

'They're coming over! I'm going.' She shot off.

Colette and the boy came across to where Anna and her mother sat. Anna could sense her mother shifting uneasily on her chair. Everybody in the room seemed to be watching. It was like the new freaks singling out the resident freaks. Thanks.

'Hi, Anna!' said Colette. 'I'm glad you're here. I wasn't sure there would be anyone I knew.'

Colette, I come to see you up in Sneck Cottage making pots. I don't want you coming down here, dressed like that, and coming over to talk to me.

'Oh, hi, Colette.'

'Anna, I want you to meet – ' and she pulled him so he stood in front of her, her hands on his shoulders, 'my son. Wolf.'

'Oh, hi!' said Anna.

His eyes moved constantly, settling briefly on Anna, her mother, then flickering round the room, looking for a way out. Anna stared at him. Your turn, Wolf. But he didn't speak.

'Oh, this is my mum,' said Anna.

'Hello. I can't call you "Anna's mum", can I?' laughed Colette.

'I'm Cath,' her mother laughed nervously.

'Can I get you a drink?' asked Colette

Wolf shook his head. Neither Anna nor her mother wanted anything and Colette strode over to the bar. The way she parted the group of men standing at the bar, she could have been a pair of scissors in her jeans. They eyed her up as she passed and grinned at each other.

'It's the dance they have once a year,' explained Anna to Wolf for something to say. 'It's pathetic, isn't it?'

Wolf didn't reply, didn't even nod. He stared at the roomful of people as if he'd just landed from Mars.

If this May Day Dance was never forgotten by Anna it certainly wasn't because of Wolf's conversation.

Short black hair, a permanent slight frown, badly-bitten fingernails, and, suggesting a confidence he didn't seem to have, an earring. Close up she could see he was older than she'd thought – fifteen, sixteen even – but he was small for his age. Weren't wolves meant to be big hairy things that ripped your guts out with one bite? Cedric would have been a better name for this worried-looking guy.

Colette came back with her drink and started making conversation with Anna's mother. It made Anna nervous to listen, so she tried talking to Wolf.

'I'm Anna. You can say hello if you want.'

He stared at her.

'Don't worry, I'm only making conversation.'

A ghost of a smile.

'I'm Wolf.'

'Where d'you live?'

He looked at her suspiciously.

'What d'you mean? Here. Colette's.'

'I mean usually. Nobody chooses to live in Whin, nobody with any sense.'

'Here. I'm going to stay at Colette's.' He spoke quietly and with a slight foreign accent.

'So when did you come here?'

'Today.'

God, this was hard work.

'So where have you been living?'

Again, the frown deepened.

'Who wants to know?'

'Well, not me. Honestly, I couldn't care less.' Here she was, working her butt off to get him to talk, and he treated her like she was the Gestapo.

Some women were finally getting up to dance; no men yet. Rachel and her mates walked by, staring and smirking at Anna and Wolf. Diarmid and Declan came to have a laugh too; Anna gave them the finger. When she turned to Wolf he was staring at her so intently it shocked her.

'Berlin,' said Wolf.

'Sorry?'

'I said, Berlin. That's where I've been staying. But no more. Things happened.'

He stared straight at the floor now. What things?

'Berlin?' asked Anna, for something to say.

'Germany. My father's still there.'

'Snap. Well, Manchester, not Berlin, but same difference.'

'Sorry?'

She heard Colette ask her mother if she wanted to dance. Her mother bit her lip and stood up.

'Look after my bag, Anna.'

And they took to the floor, her mother with her tight little wiggle, elbows tucked in, and Colette with this expressive hippy dance, arms everywhere so her jacket opened out.

Everyone was watching. Aaargh! This was seriously embarrassing, even if it was Colette they were looking at rather than her mother.

Wolf's mobile rang. He glanced at Anna, tried to make himself heard over the music, then went outside with it.

As soon as the record ended, Colette came over.

'Where's Wolf?'

'On his mobile; he went out so's he could hear.'

Colette relaxed.

'You'll get used to him, Anna.'

She went back to dance.

Oh, will I? Perhaps I'm not bothered about getting used to him, Colette.

Wolf was gone ages. Colette and Anna's mother danced to a couple more records, then Anna's mother went over to Brian and Colette came and sat down with Anna. She told Anna it would be his father who was ringing. 'They're very close,' she said. Anna wondered if this was somehow a criticism of *her* dad. Not in Berlin, he isn't very close, she thought, it's further than Manchester. No way will Wolf's dad be coming over next week.

They watched Glenn and his mates getting more drunk. Anna pointed out the people who passed for personalities in Whin and bitched about them. Jimmy Tat, the village postman, came over and asked Colette for a dance. She smiled and agreed. Anna wasn't so sure this was a good idea.

According to Brian, Jimmy Tat had seen her doing

36

early morning yoga exercises in a leotard, 'one of those all-in-one thingies' was how Brian reported it. And anyone who called themselves Ms and did early morning exercises dressed like that was, well, what did they expect?

Jimmy's mates had obviously been primed to expect something. They looked at each other and grinned as Jimmy tried to get close and wrap an arm round Colette. She pulled his hand off her two or three times, getting more annoyed each time. Then she just stopped dancing and came and sat down. Jimmy went back to his friends. They gave him a little cheer.

'Arsehole!' said Colette.

'I could have told you that,' said Anna.

But she couldn't have told Colette the next thing that happened.

Wolf came in the door, pale-faced, a trail of black from each nostril. As he came nearer, they could see it wasn't black of course, it was deep red. He was bleeding. In the doorway behind him, Glenn was shouting.

'If you touch her again, I'll kill you. Bastard!'

Hey! This wasn't real. The May Day Dance was drunk fathers and bored grannies. It wasn't small, dark strangers dribbling blood across the dance floor.

A small crowd gathered round Glenn; a space cleared round Wolf, apart from his mother who ran over, put an arm round his head, the blood running down her cream linen jacket, and without speaking a word, took him straight out of the hall. She didn't even look at the people in the doorway as she walked out, just cradled Wolf's head in her arm.

Nobody spoke. 'Hi ho silver lining' was the record playing, whatever that meant.

The mother and son disappeared into the night.

9

Anna lay in bed watching her clock blinking out a row of zeros. The more she thought about what had happened the odder it was.

In one way it was quite simple. Glenn was drunk, and a tearful Rachel claimed that Wolf had 'done something' but it wasn't clear whether he had looked at her, touched her, or even completely ignored her – which might be 'doing something' in Rachel's book.

Anna wondered whether it was actually Glenn who had 'done something' – and Anna guessed what that might have been, tonight or earlier – and a worried Rachel was finding someone else to blame. At the very least Rachel could have been winding up Glenn to prove himself on her behalf. So far, so pathetic.

Wolf was a bit of an oddball, but Anna was quite prepared to believe he hadn't even glanced at Rachel. After all, he hadn't taken much of an interest in Anna, so why should he bother with Rachel? In fact, from the look of him, he didn't care about girls at all. Oddball he might be, but Anna took his side, and Colette's, because that put her on their side against the village. Or at least against the people who had been in the village hall that night. From the things Anna heard, they had it in for Colette as well as Wolf.

Fancy piece! Who does she think she is?/Did you see those jeans, well!/On his bloody mobile; little stuck-up git./Did you notice he wouldn't look you in the eye? And where did he come from all of a sudden? Where's he been hiding?/The way she danced; I didn't know where to look!/Poor Cath, why did she pick on you? What had you done to her to get dragged up like that?/Poor Rachel, you all right, girl?/Yeah, 'course you're upset, Glenn, but cool it now, you've sorted it, mate ...

And so on; what a bunch! In only one or two faces did Anna see any hint there was any unhappiness or shame about what had happened – her mother of course, and one or two others, but they weren't saying anything, just thinking about it and wanting to get home.

But what she couldn't understand was how Colette had dealt with it. If she'd been Colette she'd have walked straight up to Glenn and hit him right in his stupid face. Just after hitting Jimmy Tat right in his stupid face. Why had Colette just collected her son without even trying to find out what it was all about? Why had she just put her arm round him – Anna could still see the blood running down that lovely cream jacket – and got him out of there as quickly as possible? OK, she wanted to defend him – but it was funny too, that someone of Wolf's age would put up with his mother doing that. In private, just about, but with people watching?

What Anna couldn't shake off was the feeling that Colette had half expected Wolf to get caught up in something and she was rushing him out before he did something else! Weird.

What wasn't weird was hearing her mother's voice in the next bedroom railing at the drunk Brian. She couldn't hear the words, just the unhappy pattern it made, and the gaps left for him to reply and he didn't.

Anna covered her ears and watched the clock blink out its green numbers. Tomorrow she'd go up to Sneck Cottage and show whose side she was on. She sent herself to sleep by trying to think of another palindrome. It was a silly game, but it would be good to take a new one up to Colette.

10

When she woke she didn't know if she'd thought of the name 'Eve' in her sleep or before, but she was pleased with it. There was something satisfying about it; it linked her, Anna, to the first woman ever.

There was no one at Sneck Cottage. The car was gone and the curtains were open; they must have got up early. Anna trailed back home and read last month's *J17*, again. No one was speaking.

She went up twice more during the day, but there was no one there. She wrote a note.

> *Dear Colette and Wolf,*
> *I've been up THREE times and your not here though you probably know that! I'm sorry about last night though it wasn't my fault. I hope your alright Wolf, Glenn is stupid stupid stupid.*
> *I will come up to see you tomorrow after school.*
> *Your friend, Anna*
> *PS I've got another palin-whatsit!*

She took it up to Sneck Cottage in the evening. Nothing had changed. The cottage was so quiet it was spooky.

There was no one there the day after, or the day after that. He'd said he was coming to live at Colette's permanently, so where was he? Surely he couldn't be in hospital, could he?

On Wednesday the car was back, but no one came to the door.

Anna was getting fed up. Was it her fault what had happened at the dance? Well, if they didn't want to see her they could take a running jump.

11

Come the weekend and Brian had an announcement: the pink Chevrolet was finally fixed! It had taken another visit from two council men, who presented Brian with a letter that said if vehicle registration number whatever it was wasn't moved by such and such a date then it would be towed away and the owner, Mr Brian McAnus, would be charged with the cost of towing.

When Brian noticed they'd spelt his name wrong he went to the door and yelled at the council men as they were getting into their car.

'Who's this? McAnus? Is that meant to be some sort of cheap crack? Come back here, you bastards! I'll give you McAnus, you can shove it up your – '

Not wise, thought Anna. That day Brian got a new nickname in the village.

But the letter got him moving. There was a week of swearing, bleeding knuckles and peering into the engine with Bill who owned the village garage and was Brian's boss. He looked doubtful. He sometimes gave Brian a sideways glance as if he were an alien species.

But, hand it to him, there he is today saying it's ready and they're all going for a run out to Boltby in it, do some shopping.

'Brian, you're sure everything's legal?'

'Go and look at the tax disc if you don't believe me, Cath. Of course it's legal; d'you think I'd make myself a sitting duck for the law? Just go and get in it, all of you.'

Anna sat behind Brian, alongside the twins. The seat was real leather and hot from the sun.

Brian said, 'The radio's not fixed yet, so how's about a quick burst of you-know-what. To say ta ra.' And as the engine rattled into life they all sang. Even Anna joined in, she felt so good.

We're on our way in the Chevrolet.
Goodbye to being a loner.
Every day in the Chevrolet
We're going to hit that homer.

One of the twins added 'Simpson' for the laugh, but Brian didn't seem to mind. 'Give the street a wave, gang!' he said.

They moved off, waving at a deserted Windermere Grove.

At the end of the street, the engine died.

After ten minutes of sitting there and listening to Brian cursing under the bonnet, they got out and trailed back to the house. Half an hour later Brian went and got the pick-up truck and towed the pink Chevrolet up to the garage. *We're on our way.* Huh!

'D'you think he'll mind if we catch the bus down? It's due soonish.' The Happy Hopper came up to Whin twice a day from Boltby. Anna thought the driver always looked glad to drive out of the village.

'Perhaps, Mum, it doesn't matter if he minds. What

45

are we supposed to do?'

'Well, he's made all that effort.'

'Any normal person wouldn't waste their time with a forty-year-old, pink, American dinosaur. Lucky us; talk about the short straw.'

'Twins! How about – ?'

But they were already upstairs, installed on the computer.

Just before they went for the bus, Anna's mother made her shout to see if they wanted to come. Declan came to the top of the stairs.

'Don't want to come, but guess what?' he said.

'What?'

'Whin's on the net. Twice. It's a gorse bush.'

'What?'

'There's a picture.' Declan waved a print-out. 'It's a sort of thorn bush.'

'Wow! So for this we're missing the bus?'

'And there's another website about Whin I've just found – '

'Declan, we've got to go. Are you coming?'

'No. Not bothered.'

'OK. We'll get over it! Don't burn the place down,' Anna shouted as she ran out. 'Second thoughts, do!'

Traffic. People. Shops. A choice of shops, the stores everyone knew about and others that looked dodgy, unknown territory. And people, people she didn't know, strangers! Old folk, mothers with buggies, a kid in a doorway asking for spare change with a dog on a bit of string, kids her age hanging out – but a few steps ahead in sophistication. She was losing it, up in Whin; she'd have to sharpen up.

And this was only Boltby, for God's sake!

Anna and Cath shopped together. Your mother couldn't wear exactly the same things; thirty-two is like, well, old, but from the end of the shop you could imagine it was your older sister. You couldn't have done that with Rachel's mother.

The sheer fun stupidity of it, holding this top up, pulling a face at that one, laughing behind people's backs – *She's not serious about that, is she? God!* – going to another shop and then coming back to try it on again, being amazed at that price, perhaps buying.

After a couple of hours they collapsed into a café. The waitress was from Anna's school, the year above. They never spoke normally and now did fake *Hiyas* at each other.

'Just tea, please. Or are we allowed a cake, Anna?'

'Big day out; let's go for it! Oh, and make sure it's ordinary tea, not that China stuff,' said Anna.

'You what?' asked the waitress.

Obviously went to the same charm school as Rachel.

'Two teas, and what cakes have you got?' Glancing down at the waitress's slightly bulging hips Anna added, 'We don't care about the calorie count.'

Unfair, but you have to get some practice in.

And then, looking across the tables, Anna saw Colette St John. She was reading a book.

No Wolf, though.

Had she heard the China tea thing? She must have. But Anna had only said it for something to say, she hadn't meant it, or at least hadn't meant it to hurt. In any case, why should she bother about upsetting Colette? Where had she been for the past week?

Colette looked up, and smiled at her.

'Oh, it's your friend – Colette,' said her mother.

Colette stood up and came across, bringing her cup and book.

'Hi! Can I join you?'

She sat down anyway. She was wearing the cream jacket, and even though it had been cleaned Anna thought she could see a faint stain where the blood had been.

'Been shopping?' asked Colette. 'Let's have a look at what you've got, then.'

Miserably, because she knew what Colette St John would think of them, Anna showed her the skimpy, spangly top and the new shoes with the incredible heels.

'Nice!' said Colette, though surely she didn't mean it. 'I'm just going up to the village. Can I offer you a lift?'

Anna and her mother looked at each other.

'No, we haven't finished yet,' lied Anna.

'I can wait.'

'It's OK.'

Colette looked at her for a moment, wondering, then, changing the subject. said brightly: 'I never asked you what work you did, Cath.'

'Oh, hairdressing. It's only part-time really.'

'You shouldn't apologise – it's a useful job. People

need their hair doing.'

'Yeah, but anyone can do it, there's thousands of hairdressers. Not like what you do, that's different.'

'What you do is artistic in its own way – I'm sure all hairdressers are different, too. Besides, there's thousands of us making pots. It's just a job like yours, Cath.'

'I suppose so.' Her mother didn't sound convinced. 'What's the book?'

'Oh, it's just trash. Good fun, though. What are you reading? Do you read?'

'No, not really.'

And silence. This was her mum, who chatted to all her customers as easily and naturally as her hands did their job – people came for the chat as much as the hairdo. She was in awe of Colette and became awkward. She sounded stupid. What was terrible for Anna was seeing her mum as Colette saw her, as some brainless bimbo hairdresser with nothing to talk about.

'Coming up to see me sometime, Anna?'

No mention of Wolf, or the dance, or where they'd been, or Anna's note, or anything. Whose job was it to bring it up?

'Er, yes. I came up last week.'

'Oh, I've been away,' said Colette vaguely. 'Come up; it'll be nice to see you. We can make some pots.'

'OK. How's Wolf?'

'He's fine. I'd sooner not talk about him, if you don't mind. He's gone away for a while.'

But I'm your friend, there's no one else in the village.

Why are you talking to me like this?

'I'll be off,' said Colette.

She stood up, and then suddenly stooped and gave Anna a kiss on her cheek. As Colette turned to leave, Anna rubbed it off with the back of her hand.

12

When they got home there was a message from Anna's dad.

Anna? Sorry, pet, the car thing can't happen for a bit, my mate I was borrowing it from wrote it off last week so I can't lend it because it's...written off. Sorry about that. Anybody there? I was with him when he did it and let's say I'm glad to be able to make this call. Barmy bastard. By the way, Cath, we need to have a chat about money, doesn't have to be a long chat, there isn't much to say. You guessed it. Sorry again, Anna, but I'll tell you what –
Screech.

Oh, Dad, Dad, you're hopeless. Useless. Gripless. Brainless. And daughterless too, soon, if you don't do something about it. No, I don't mean that.

But is it so difficult, seeing me once in a while? You obviously see your mates all the time. And why keep ringing up to promise this and that and then not showing. I wish you just didn't bother at all, just don't bother ringing at all. No, I don't mean that.

Anna sat and fumed.

She couldn't rely on her dad. She couldn't rely on her new friend, who seemed to think she could pretend to be all equal and adult, but then turn Anna off when she felt like it.

And she certainly couldn't rely on the son, who thinks he can appear from nowhere, say almost nothing to make himself interesting, and then disappear again. And nobody thinks they owe her an explanation.

Well, if she couldn't get back at her dad she could at Colette St John. Tired of the little concerned looks her mother kept giving her, Anna went up to Sneck Cottage.

She came to the door as soon as Anna knocked.

'You don't have to knock, Anna; you know that.'

'Well, I don't know what I know. Like, did you get my note?'

Colette looked down.

'I'm sorry. Yes. Thank you. I should have got in touch sooner.'

Anna shrugged. 'It's OK. I suppose.'

'I need to explain things. D'you want a drink? "That China stuff", perhaps?' She smiled.

'Sorry. I didn't mean it, not really.' God, she shouldn't be the one apologising!

'Here. Have some juice.' And she brought two glasses of cloudy apple juice to the table.

Colette said: 'When I was a kid I thought adults had it all sorted. But we don't, you know, we make it up as we go along, too.' She paused. 'I need to tell you about Wolf.'

And because she stopped and didn't seem to know what to say next, Anna asked: 'Why did you call him that? Perhaps if you'd called him "Tom" or something he'd have melted into the background more. Perhaps not got hit.'

'I don't see his name's any reason to pick on him!' said Colette sharply, then paused to let her anger subside. 'I was heavily into Mozart when I had him.'

'You what?'

'Mozart, the composer; his first name was Wolfgang, and we were living in Germany at the time. It didn't seem so crazy. It's only a name.'

'I suppose. So where is he now?'

'With his father. Back in Berlin. It was only for the weekend he was here.'

But didn't Wolf tell Anna he'd left Berlin for good to stay with Colette? She stared at Anna, as if daring her to contradict.

'And it didn't turn out so good,' said Colette. 'At the dance.'

'No. But you shouldn't have gone like that. They'd have come round. They only need telling where to get off.'

'I don't think we should have to wait for them to come round, Anna. Wolf did nothing wrong.'

'No, but that's what they're like. You have to stand up to them.'

'I don't want to expose Wolf to those bastards,' the venom coming back into Colette's voice.

'Fair enough. But that's what they're like.'

Why was she having to give Colette lessons in how to get on with arseholes? Who was meant to be the one with experience here?

'So you've got a kid and he lives with his dad.' Anna felt a little knot in her throat as she said it. 'Hardly a big deal these days.'

'No, I suppose not.'

'Did you want him here, is that it?'

'Of course. It's new to me, him not being around.'

'Why did you come to Whin? Did you pick it off the map, with a pin?'

'Not quite,' she laughed, 'I have one or two contacts round here, friends. In Manchester, not in the village of course.'

'No, you wouldn't have. Dressing funny, going in the pub on your own, reading books in there; Brian tells us all about it.'

'Shall I say, I have been in more welcoming places. Apart from you, of course. And your mother's been very friendly.' Colette smiled at Anna. 'It's good to have someone to talk to. There've been problems. You've seen how dark Wolf is, so he gets racist comments at school. A couple of months ago he was beaten up.'

'Shit!'

'We're thinking of taking him out of school. Anybody with any talent just gets picked on.'

'So does he do pottery, then? Is he artistic?'

'Yes, he does pottery. And we're all artists, Anna.'

'Oh yeah. Except your pots are loads better than mine, and I bet Wolf's are too.'

'You only need time to develop,' said Colette, but Anna knew she didn't really mean it.

'If he's sixteen he can leave school,' said Anna. 'I

would.'

'He's only just sixteen. He needs his own space.'

Colette paused and looked at Anna.

'Anna, I haven't told you everything. I can trust you to keep this to yourself? I'm sorry to ask but – '

Anna nodded, frowning at Colette. She took a breath.

'Six months ago Wolf was accused – the daughter of German friends of ours accused Wolf of assaulting her, of – of – ' Colette stopped and took a deep breath. 'As good as raping her.'

'Wow!'

'We got different versions of course; we don't know what really happened. Wolf said this, Steffi said that. We wanted it sorting out without going to the police; we hated the law, all that, we thought it would only make things worse. But her parents were ultra-respectable, very upset. They wanted to do everything by the book, even though we thought they were making a mountain out of a molehill. Steffi just seemed confused about... whatever it was that happened. But how could going to the courts help?' Colette appealed to Anna. 'Social workers, probation officers, people like that; how could they make anything better for Wolf, or Steffi?'

Anna couldn't think what to say; this was all too new, scary even.

'Anyway,' continued Colette, 'perhaps you can see why we didn't stay around when he got hit at the bloody village dance. Poor Wolf; his first night over from Germany. The main reason we came over to England was for a bit of peace and quiet, a bit of space. Fat chance.'

The unhappy Colette was back. Not so sorted.

'Poor kid,' said Anna.

'Sometimes we think he's got over it – '

'And what was she called, Steffi?'

'I think he's got over her.'

'No, I meant it must have been horrible for her.'

Colette glared at her.

'What do you mean, horrible?'

What had she said wrong? Obviously Wolf was the only important one in all this.

Colette said, 'I'm sorry, perhaps I shouldn't have told you all this, to have expected you to be able to understand – I mean you're only a kid but there's really no one else to talk to in this godforsaken – little – '

Now Colette began to cry and Anna watched in horror for a minute before she awkwardly reached out and patted Colette's deathly white hand with clay dust round the fingernails.

Anna stayed all evening and listened to Colette talk, about her own childhood as the daughter of a diplomat trailing round the world, about going to art school and learning to be a potter, about meeting her husband, Yannis, who was Greek, about what a quiet child Wolf had been and how they had to protect him from other kids, about Wolf talking less and less in spite of their efforts to 'get his feelings in the open'.

So the mystery of why she swept Wolf out of the village hall was solved. And what had Wolf said about Berlin? *Things happened.* Talk about understatement of the century.

Except. *Two* girls accusing Wolf was starting to look like a pattern, even a habit. OK; Rachel making accusations at the dance was one thing, but what about this Steffi? How could Anna make her mind up about that?

Thank God Wolf was back in Berlin.

As the evening dragged on, Anna began to hear in what Colette was saying a constant refrain: Where had they gone wrong? How could they put it right? Could Anna help her understand what had happened? It was as if Colette was asking Anna to explain the world to her.

It was awful. Anna wanted back the competent person who knew interesting things and taught her to make pots, not this bag of misery. Give me the twins behaving like dorks, Rachel with her gormless mates, even Brian drunk, but take me away from Colette who wants more than I can give her. I'm only a fourteen-year-old kid, give us a break!

13

Anna's mother wanted to decorate the house that summer.

'The place is a complete tip, I can't stand it.'

'We're not allowed to decorate, it's a council house,' said Brian.

Neat way to avoid a job.

'Brian,' her mother said sweetly, 'the council can take a running jump. And so can the rest of you – I'll do it on my own if I have to. In fact I'd sooner do it on my own. Starting Monday. OK?'

Well, this was progress! But the practical details of where to start and what would be needed and how much it would cost all began to overwhelm her mother's original go-for-it decision, and Brian of course knew so much about the proper way to decorate.

'Brian,' said Anna, 'why don't you shut up? – You're not even doing it, Mum is, we are. And can we start with my room?'

'Oh yeah! D'you know which end of a brush to hold? Sure, you'll be a great help. That's when you're here and not up at bloody Sneck Cottage. You just about live there!'

'What would you know about?' said Anna. 'We all know where you live. The Bull.'

'Anna! Leave it out!' said her mother.

'Well, it'd certainly make things better down here, if you moved in with her,' Brian said. As soon as he'd said it he gave Cath a guilty glance and looked down.

Anna gave his bald patch a look of pure hatred.

'I just wish you two could get on. Make life easier, not harder.' Anna's mother's eyes were moist.

'Yeah, well, he's your boyfriend, not mine.'

So even before school ended Anna's mother started turning the house upside down, and Anna found herself spending evenings and weekends up at Sneck Cottage with its cool rooms, small windows letting in bright oblongs of sunlight on the bare floorboards, the white walls with Indian wall hangings. She didn't think too much about what her mother might be feeling about it.

When she got home from school she'd try sunbathing out the front at Windermere Grove. The grass was waist high, but she put down a towel, hung her top on the spade, and lay down on the towel. The sun warmed her back, the grass made a den round her, and all she could hear were insect noises and the Phillipses' stone boy peeing endlessly into their pond. But then there'd be giggling from upstairs and chewed up paper pellets thrown or water pistols squirted and she'd have to give up, and after another foul mealtime she'd want out. Her mother didn't say she couldn't.

Anna also had a job.

The landlord at The Bull told Brian they needed someone to wash up at weekend lunch times – 'It'll be a bit of pocket money for your lass'. Brian said yes on

Anna's behalf.

'Thanks a bunch,' said Anna.

'I thought I was doing you a favour – you could do with the cash, couldn't you?'

'How much?'

It turned out to be £3 an hour for scrubbing out pans and oven trays that the dishwasher wouldn't touch. That was the easy bit. The drawback was having to work with Lydia.

At first Anna thought Lydia was an oddball character, the sort you get in a bad TV soap to add some interest. She did things her way. The kitchen of The Bull was her empire.

'Them baking trays, they live up there,' she told Anna, putting her right.

'It's too high.'

'That's where they live. You'll soon learn, Anne.'

'Anna. I'll put them in here, where I can reach?'

'Well, thank you for just walking in and sorting us out! Put them where I said.'

'Sorry.' Apologising didn't come easy, even harder when it wasn't you who was wrong.

'There's more to this job than you think. They don't last long, the lasses what work here. There's been two already come and gone this year. I don't think you'll last either, Anne.'

By the end of her first session with Lydia, Anna realised two things about those soap opera oddballs. On TV you only get them for a minute at a time, and they only exist to annoy the rest of the characters.

But the money in her hand was a real tenner, a pound over for the three hours she'd worked.

'Call it quits,' said the landlord, and patted her bum.

She only saw Rachel on the school bus. Rachel was spending the daytime hanging around with two younger girls and the evenings with Glenn. The tickling and wrestling games seemed to have stopped, so perhaps Anna's theory that they were doing more than kissing was true. They looked completely miserable. Called 'growing up', thought Anna. They might as well get used to it, if they can't think of anything else to do.

Once she bumped into Rachel when she was taking Brian's lunch round to the garage for him; her mother was busy decorating.

'You skiving off school too?' asked Anna.

'What's it look like?' said Rachel.

'Yeah, it's not worth going in hardly.'

'Left home, have you?' asked Rachel.

'No, why?'

'You seem to be nearly living up at Sneck. What it looks like to me. Not that I care.'

Anna said nothing.

'You and Muzz Toilet. And the Wolf boy.'

'Sorry to disappoint you but there's only Colette. The Wolf's in Berlin with his dad.'

'Best place too.'

Brian came to the door, lighting a cigarette with a welding torch. Impressive.

'Thanks, Anna. What're we on today?'

'I dunno. Whatever it is that grows in sandwiches. Have a look.'

In the dark at the back of the garage she could see the Chevrolet. There was a sheet over the bonnet and black metal things on the sheet. It was being used as a worktop. Crazy but hopeful outside the house, it now looked derelict. It wasn't going anywhere soon.

There was a pin-up calendar on the wall. Anna stared fascinated at the near-naked model glistening in the heat or perhaps because she'd been covered in engine oil. If Anna was going to look like that, she'd have to get a move on! But of course it was impossible. Being an adult was impossible, and it was worse being a kid.

Her life was at a complete standstill. What was she going to find to do in the holiday when it came? Wolf had been a bit of excitement – lasting all of two hours – and now there was only Sneck Cottage and Colette.

The Colette who had cried on Anna's shoulder had disappeared; the familiar Colette – in charge, a bit snooty, funny – was back. She didn't talk about Wolf.

Anna was getting better at making pots.

'Can I fire this one, Colette?'

'Why not? Then you can have a go at glazing it.'

And Colette cut Anna's bowl from the wheel with the wire and lifted it onto a board. It was a bit thick and the curve of it wasn't quite what she'd planned. Still, she was getting control of the clay and that felt good. Anna picked it up to take it to the kiln.

'Oh, Anna,' said Colette, sharply, pointing to a side room, 'I've had the kiln moved into the scullery, through there.'

'What for?'

Colette shrugged and said vaguely: 'It's better than having to cross the yard. The weather could be bad.'

Anna frowned. It could be, but it isn't, not just now. It's solid sun out there. She took her bowl into the scullery, where the kiln took up too much space and Colette's pots seemed crowded together, like those hundreds of Chinese warriors Anna had just seen on a travel programme.

14

Dear Dad,

Well how are you what have you been up to? It must of been terrible being in that car smash with your friend. Scary! Isn't there someone else you can borrow a car off of? Or why don't you come over on the bus, Mum says there's nothing stopping you she says your 'more than welcome' her words. I could meet you in Boltby if you didn't want to come up to Whin. Which I could quite understand!!!!!

Well there's nothing much new here. Mum's been decorating the house like mad – all of it!! Lazy guts Brian hasn't helped just criticises the way she does it. As for the twins – don't ask. They sit there at the computer zap zap zap all day. If mum had painted them along with the walls they probably wouldnt of noticed.

I've got a job working in the bull at weekends. The moneys rubbish and it makes my hands itch. Brian says there's a law that I should have rubber gloves. The things he says. A rubber glove law!

Sometimes I go up to my friends house Colette if you can call her a friend she's older than mum. She makes pottery and shes new to the village. Shes a hippy I suppose and has done loads of dead interesting things. She's got a son called Wolf!!!! Who is meant to have *done something criminal I can't tell you about but he lives in Berlin thats Germany with his dad. Perhaps I'll tell you more when I can talk to you it'll be alright because you don't live in the village.*

Brian has just asked me what I'm doing so I've told him so hes said 'tell Michael he's to come over to the Bar-B-Cue we're having on Saturday'. What Bar-B-Cue? First I've heard about it. Anyway, I've told you now. And now he's gone back to watching the TV, scratching his armpits under his T-shirt. I can hear it – ITS HORRIBLE!!!!

Dad I dont really want to write a letter it's not talking to you properly. I'm only doing it this way because Mum suggested it. Why dont you ring or come over. Why dont you say when I can come over there? But I dont want to sound like Im criticising because I'm sure youve got good reasons.

Well thats all for now. RING ME UP!!!

Hugs and kisses,

Anna

(your daughter remember!)

15

There *was* a barbecue on Saturday. Brian had come up with the idea off the top of his head in the club and all his friends were definitely coming and bringing their wives. But telling Anna was the first mention of it at home.

Her mother said, 'We haven't even got a barbecue, Brian.'

'Easy. I'll rig something up from some scrap metal round at the garage. And they sell that charcoal down at Asda.'

'And all the food – are we providing that?'

'God, woman! A few sausages, a bit of chicken – what's the problem?'

'But you reckon there's how many coming? All your mates you said.'

'Yes, well, half a dozen sausages should do it,' said Anna.

'Shut it, you,' said Brian. 'You'll see.'

So the barbecue was going to happen. Colette got asked too.

Brian brought home this thing he'd made at work out of, Anna supposed, bits of dead cars. He stood it out the back and they all had to go out and admire it. It was like a modern sculpture.

'Where do we put the charcoal?' asked Cath.

'In there, obviously,' said Brian.

'And what about the meat?'

'There's going to be a rack on those bits that stick out.'

'But it'll never cook that far away from the heat!'

'Mum, if Brian wants to give the village salmonella, why should we stop him?' said Anna.

It was Brian's big event. He borrowed Bill's car to go down to the supermarket and spent the week's housekeeping on bags of charcoal, packets of skewers, trays of pale pink meat and cans of beer.

He had a trial run at Friday teatime, piling charcoal into the Brian-B-Cue, as Anna and her mum had christened it, and using the acetylene torch from the garage to get the whole thing smouldering.

'Don't bother with tea, Cath,' he said, carrying one of the trays of meat out of the back door, 'I'll do it.'

But an hour later he was still anxiously poking at the chicken pieces and turning them over for the zillionth time.

'I'll open a tin of beans for the twins, Brian.'

The twins were on the ground, doing dying-of-hunger impressions.

'We said that rack was too high. It'll never cook,' said Anna.

Brian shouted at them, 'If you'd all just stop bothering me, I could get on a lot faster.'

'It could hardly be a lot slower,' muttered Anna to her mother as they trooped back in. They had beans. Sometime later Brian brought the chicken in. One of the twins made clucking noises. Brian threw it down on the

67

table and stormed off to the pub.

The barbecue had disaster written all over it. No one would come and if they did they'd only get food poisoning. Anna didn't even think Colette would come; she seemed to have too much on her mind. She was also working hard, busy whenever Anna went up. She was probably working now; Anna could see the lights of the cottage at the top of the field. The outside lights were on, and a fainter light glimmered in the outhouse too.

But everything started fine on Saturday, including the weather. Brian spent the morning modifying the Brian-B-Cue so the food would cook. Bill arrived, apologising for his wife who he said wasn't feeling so good. Anna was wrong about Colette, too; she came bang on time, dressed in this multi-coloured sack thing, and tried to make conversation with the twins who were eating their way through the crisps.

The phone rang.

'Is Brian there?'

'Dad!'

'Hi, pet, is that you?'

'You're not coming, are you?'

'Sorry, I was just ringing to let Brian know I couldn't but thanks for the invite. It's today, isn't it?'

'Right now. You got my letter, then?'

'Yes, thanks, Anna, it was brilliant, I can't tell you, getting an envelope – I mean, no one ever writes to me – and in your handwriting.'

'Feel free to write back.'

'Ha ha. Well, I might just do that, I might just. Tell you what, pet, I'm in a bit of a rush, is Brian there?'

Outside Brian was using some sort of flame-thrower on the charcoal. Bill and Colette were talking to each other but watching Brian nervously.

'He's busy right now, doing circus tricks.'

'Oh? Never mind, same old Anna. Don't ever change, will you?'

'I might just, I'm warning you.'

'Ha ha. Got to go, pet. Tell your mother I rang, and say hello to the IRA from me.'

'No. 'Bye, Dad.'

'Ha ha.'

Click.

A problem had come up; Colette was a vegetarian. Anna knew but had forgotten to tell anyone. So it was her fault. Colette insisted it wasn't a problem and she would have some salad, that was fine.

Then the sky clouded over. Two more of Brian's friends from the club came, both without their wives, though one of them had two young sons who sat and watched TV with the twins because it was getting cold outside.

No one else came.

The four men drank beer and joked, Brian occasionally prodding the cooking meat. Cath and Colette and Anna stood around getting goosebumps on their bare arms. After poking at some lettuce and tomato for a while Colette said she had to go. She gave Anna a thin, sad smile and a hug, and left.

Anna went upstairs and lay on her bed. Everything was just too sad. Why had no one come to the barbecue? And for those who had come, why had it clouded over?

Brian shouted, 'It's at the top of the stairs, lads.' And two of the men clumped upstairs into the toilet together, leaving the door open.

'Room for a little one?' asked one and they chuckled. Their peeing made a tremendous noise, like cows doing it.

Then one said: 'McAnus and his bloody barbecue; what did we come for?'

'Aye, the rest of them had the right idea, keep well away,' said the other.

'His wife's OK, in fact she's nice – '

The other gave a mucky laugh.

' – but what's she doing with him? The man's one hundred per cent total bollocks. It's been nothing but arguments in the club since he started coming in. The oppressed Irish this and the bloody British state the other. You just don't need it.'

Anna held her breath and listened. They were a bit drunk but this was the truth she was hearing.

'And that bloody pink Cadillac – '

'Chevrolet.'

'Whatever. Making the whole street look untidy. And I'll tell you what, I bet that bloody barbecue'll still be there in a year's time for the neighbours to look at.'

'I don't know how she puts up with it, what's she called, Cath. And the daughter hates him, they say.'

'Mind you, she's in no position. Snooty little cow.'

70

And they flushed the toilet and went downstairs laughing.

Anna just lay on the bed for a while. Then she went over to the window and looked out. The four men had opened up another can of beer apiece. One of the men she'd just overheard now had his arm round Brian's shoulder; they were laughing together.

And for a moment, as she stared at the men standing round the smouldering Brian-B-Cue, she wanted to run down and pull that treacherous arm off Brian and put her own round him.

16

The rain had only lasted a day – specially turned on to spoil the barbecue of course – and the sun came out again, and stayed out. She'd been trying to sunbathe but as usual the twins kept pestering; Declan shouted down he wanted to show her something but it would only be some pervy little joke so she ignored him till he shut up. Then he started throwing things from the upstairs window; a paper plane sailed down. She gave up and took her towel up to the field behind Sneck Cottage, well away from everyone.

Snooty little cow.

Her head played the phrase again and again, said in the same voice and with the same laugh. The sun was hot but she had a cold, tight knot in her stomach, a mixture of outrage and hurt. Outrage because it wasn't true, she wasn't 'snooty', you could ask anybody, Rachel – well, perhaps not, or, or...

So that's what they thought, was it? Well, if they did, they did, and she didn't care! But however courageously she told herself this, that she didn't care, she knew she did.

She tried to push it out of her mind, to think nothing about anything, and just feel the sun on her skin. There was a bird directly above her, giving it plenty – a lark or something? The June sun shone full on her face; she opened her eyes a fraction to peer into the seething white hole of the sun. You could see the rays, sliding down and touching your eyelashes. Staring at the sun; you shouldn't do it but if you could outstare the sun, what couldn't you do?

What was that over by the wall?

She sat up quickly. There, where the outhouse of Sneck Cottage met the wall round the field. There were one or two creepy men in the village but there was no reason why Ratty Gifford should be right up here.

A sheep perhaps? There was nothing there. Her eyes probably, gone funny from the sun. She closed her eyes and lay back again, listening to the bird singing its heart out.

The trouble was, when she pushed one thing out of her mind, something else entered it. Wolf.

What was he? What *had* happened in Germany? Where was he now? Anna had met a scared rabbit of a kid who'd said almost nothing to her, taken phone calls all night from his father, been beaten up by the village headbanger, and then disappeared. How was that the same person who had done something horrible to a girl in Berlin and worried his mother sick? Anna couldn't get the two people into the one undersized figure with the bloodied nose she'd met at the May Day Dance, an age ago.

God – sunbathing was meant to be relaxing! The bird had shut up – no, that was it starting up again.

There *was* something over there!

She sat up. A cow over by the fence, that was all. But

she had suddenly become conscious of how bare she was, only a bikini top and a skirt. She put on her top, grabbed her towel and walked quickly down the field. She couldn't relax anyway; too much stuff churning round in her head.

On the road she met Rachel with her gormless friend, Andrea.

'So how's the romance of the century going?' asked Rachel.

'Come again?'

'You know, you and the Wolf.'

'Didn't you know? He took one look at the place and got on the next plane back to Berlin. Can't say that I blame him. I mean, it's a hard choice, Whin or Berlin, isn't it?' But as soon as she said it Anna could hear that other voice: snooty little cow.

'Like I say, Andrea,' said Rachel, 'she can't wait to get after him. He was a bit dark for me.'

'His dad's Greek.'

'He were like a Nasian,' said Andrea.

'No need to sunbathe, then, has he, Andrea?' said Anna, eyeing Andrea's peeling skin; she'd asked for it.

Anna walked off. She could hear them laughing after her. Anna tried to be friends, and just ended up being sarcastic; she couldn't help it. But to be liked by them, she would have to be like them.

On the path lay the paper plane. For no reason she picked it up, opened it out. On it was a photograph of Sneck Cottage. It was a computer print-out, but what was it for? Below the photograph it said:

WWW
WOLF'S WHIN WORLD
The wolf is Canis Lupus
The whin is Ulex Europaeus
The world is what you make it
e-mail me on wolfswhinworld@hotmail.com

And across the bottom someone had written in biro:
Off the internet – for Anna if your intrested.

This must be what Declan had wanted to show her.
Was this the stuff about the gorse bush he'd told her
about before? But he hadn't mentioned anything about
the wolf, or should that be Wolf? And what was the
picture of Sneck Cottage doing?

Was it all just some sort of joke of Declan's? He knew
about Wolf, and he knew Wolf had disappeared; he also
probably knew half the village had Wolf and Anna as
good as married off and living three doors further up
Windermere Grove. So maybe it was all just a bit of a
nerd prank.

Best say nothing. Check it out. There were still two
weeks of school left.

Anna had an idea.

17

Hey, canis lupus, arent you meant to be extinct? We've gotten wolves up in Canada and over in the Rockies, & i know 1 or 2 here in high school, but hasnt the wolf been dead in Europe for like a million years or something?

So where's your lair???!!! Tell me about you and i'll tell you about me.

The world is how you see it.

Peace.

Bananna

Anna was quite proud of it. It had been dead easy: chat up the class geek, a Harry Potter lookalike called Aaron Cowgill. She got some funny looks from her classmates when she suddenly started turning the charm on him of all people, and Aaron looked like all his birthdays had arrived together, but it worked. He showed her the one computer in the library that would do free e-mail. It was a secret, Aaron said; only he knew about it.

There were obviously many things only Aaron knew about and Anna was happy for it to stay that way, but she got him to set her up with a hotmail address. She was quite chuffed with *bananna* – it was Anna and not-Anna at the same time, and stupid too. For the message she borrowed high-school movie-speak to invent a kid from the USA. She thought *lair* was classy, though she had to look up what they called wolves' dens.

And now she had to wait and see what Wolf's Whin World had to do with Wolf.

There was no reply that day or the day after. Aaron showed her how to open her mail box and explained about time differences in different parts of the world but Anna stopped listening.

On Wednesday Aaron handed her a sheet of paper; she had mail.

'Hey!' she said: 'What happened to privacy?'

'Sorry. But, like, you need me to get into it anyway.'

Aaron blinked behind his Harry Potters like she might hit him, but he'd still be glad of the attention. She grabbed the e-mail and went to the toilet to read it.

From: canis lupus <wolfswhinworld@hotmail.com>
To: bananna<bananna@hotmail.com>
Subject: howl
Date: 20 June 2001 11.23

'The world is what you make it' wasn't my idea. Let's say someone chose it for me.

The world is how you see it? You're right – let me tell you how I see it.

In my room I've got 2 windows. One of them is Windows – you know, Microsoft's Windows – and that's what I'm looking through now. It's a computer and things come in through it and things go out through – but it's not real enough, you know?

My other window is a real window – it's small but I can look out at the village I live in. I suppose you'd have to call it living. I used to live in Berlin but now I live on the edge of a small village in the North of England – I won't say why just now.

There's not much going on out there. Even through my telescope there's not much to see – so I look at the night sky and stuff like that.

This is my den. There's one girl who comes up to do pottery with my mother – she's nice – but I don't see her to speak to now.

Mail me back, bananna – tell me about somewhere else. Wolf

18

So much for the mystery of where Wolf was; Anna knew exactly which small village in the North of England he lived in. As soon as she got home that afternoon, she was out of the door and up the hill.

No car. She remembered. Wednesday was a craft fair day; that's where Colette would be. So Wolf would be alone.

Anna hammered on the door of the outhouse. No reply.

She went round the corner but the window was too high. In the yard were a couple of wooden crates that Colette used for packing pots in. Anna dragged one over to the window and stood on it. Because of the brilliant sunshine she had to use her hands as blinkers to see in.

She could dimly make out a few cardboard boxes, some polystyrene packing, and a couple of expensive-looking suitcases, but no kiln and no racks of pots – well, she knew where they were now. In the scullery.

The window was open slightly... Should she? No question about it.

She got the other crate, put it on the first and with a stick was able to lift up the catch and open the window all the way. She had squirmed through, scraped her arm and landed awkwardly on the other side, before she'd even worked out if this was sensible or not.

It was only a few steps up the stairs – and now she knew her guess was right. The upstairs had a single bed, unmade and obviously recently slept in. There was a clothes rack, a chest of drawers – the top one open with a black T-shirt hanging out, a small bookcase, a small desk, and on it a state-of-the-art computer. wolfswhinworld@hotmail.com. Wolf's little den nobody knew about, apart from Colette, and anybody who e-mailed him. Bananna.

At the window, the telescope. Anna got down and squinted through it. If you adjusted the focus you could look right into the front rooms of Windermere Grove. Creepy.

So now what? She could go back down the stairs, out through the window, put the crates back, and say nothing, knowing what she did. Or she could come back and confront Colette. Or she could wait for him and sort it out right now. In fact, she thought, what I would like to do – and she sat down on the bed, leaning against the wooden headboard – is put on one of those granny caps, wrap a shawl round me, and when he comes back, bite his bloody stupid timid little Wolf's head off. Little Red Riding Hood bites back.

She smiled at the idea and gazed round the room. Bright rug on the floor. A mobile hanging from the ceiling but not moving, there was no air moving at all. It was hot. She stared at the guitar leaning in the corner.

19

She woke up suddenly when a car door slammed in the yard. She sat up, but knew there was nowhere to go.

She heard Colette call: 'I'll bring your tea over in a little while, Wolfie.'

Anna now clocked the old plate and mug on the end of the desk. So that's how it worked; she brought the meals over. She was wondering where he went to the toilet when she heard the key turn in the lock and the downstairs door opened.

Anna went and sat at the desk, out of his line of vision when he appeared. She was ready.

As soon as his head appeared through the hole in the floor, she said, trying to sound as cool as she could manage: 'Hello, Wolf.'

He froze on the stair, then turned towards where she sat. He didn't speak.

'What's going on?'

Wolf just stared, then walked up the stairs and sat on the bed.

'I don't get it,' said Anna. 'You've been here all the time, haven't you?'

She stood up and went to the top of the stairs; she might want to get out quick.

He shrugged. 'It was Colette's idea. After what

happened that first night.'

'Let's start there, Wolf. What did happen at the dance?'

'That girl looked at me – '

'Rachel.'

'Is that what she's called? She smiled at me. I didn't do anything. Next thing I know her boyfriend's hitting me in the face and yelling something about me trying to "get off with her".'

'So you didn't touch her?'

'Anna; it was my first night in the village. I'd just flown in from Germany. I didn't know anybody except Colette. So no, I didn't go near her. I don't think I even smiled back.'

It was the first time he'd spoken Anna's name, and it was OK; it didn't spook her out or anything. And she didn't have any problem believing Wolf didn't smile back.

'One thing you need to learn, Wolf: Glenn is a dork. He just needs telling, that's all.'

'I've had easier introductions.'

She nodded. 'Yeah. OK. But hiding up here – I mean, are you going to do it for ever?'

He shrugged. 'See how it goes.' Then he gave her a direct look. 'How much do you know, about me?'

'Colette said something, about that girl in Germany.'

'What did she say?'

Anna said: 'It doesn't matter what she said, does it? What do *you* say?'

He stared at her. A small dark face with the beginnings of a moustache. He opened his mouth, and closed it.

'Wolf,' said Anna: 'Did you do anything to that girl you shouldn't have?'

'No.'

'Like, really?'

'No.'

Then he started.

'In Berlin we mixed with artists and writers, journalists, musicians. They were always talking about art, this movie, that exhibition. Some of them actually did that stuff, others were just on the fringes, hangers-on. There were always people round, with their kids and a bottle of wine. There'd be a new CD by someone we knew, a new gallery off Alexanderplatz, famous people who lived round the corner, like Günter Grass – '

'Yeah, well, there would be, wouldn't there?' said Anna. She didn't have a clue what he was talking about. But sarcasm didn't seem to work on Wolf. He kept talking in his soft voice, a voice that lulled you and made you listen, even when you didn't know what he was on about.

'Everything was kind of easy. Yannis went off to work every day but nobody else seemed to. It was all visiting each other's flats, staying up late talking, arguing, drinking, smoking. The kids never went to bed, we were equal, had our own ideas to express, all that.'

Was he mocking his parents' ideas, Anna wondered? His parents, who didn't want their son to call them 'Mum' and 'Dad'.

'Like, this is fascinating, Wolf, but you're not telling me what I need to know. Tell me about Steffi. About you and Steffi.'

'Steffi's parents weren't really part of the same crowd. They liked having artists for friends but when it came down to it, they were old-fashioned, respectable types. Herr Fleischmann – ' and Wolf winced as he said the name ' – was a big deal in the Bundesbank or something. I think he just wanted modern art for his office, to show everyone he was cultured. And as for Steffi's mum – well, she was the respectable wife of a big deal in the Bundesbank. Whose daughter could do no wrong.'

'A bit like Colette and her son,' Anna couldn't resist saying. 'Go on; I've got the background, Wolf, so what happened?'

A long pause.

'I don't like talking about it. It sounds like I'm blaming her, and I'm not. I don't know if she'd been reading something or seen a film, I don't think she knew what she was doing, just experimenting. And so was I. I suppose we were two kids messing around. The magazines, they have all this advice and all these details of what to do, but all I know is we were just two kids messing. And I don't even know in the end what we did, it was all new and confusing.'

'Aw, come on!'

'I really don't...' He trailed off, then, very definite: 'But I didn't force her to do anything, Anna.'

Silence. He sounded like someone telling the truth.

'It was weeks after when she said something to her mother – and all hell broke loose. Frau Fleischmann wanted to go straight to the police but Colette managed to persuade her to give us some time to try and sort it out. It went on and on: Steffi, you give your side, Wolf, what do you think happened? Steffi, what do you feel now? Wolf, what are you saying Steffi did? Steffi, where exactly...? You can't imagine, Anna, the crying, the talking, the express-your-anger, hour after hour.'

Anna remembered Colette, and thought: I can imagine.

'She's an old dragon, Steffi's mother, but she was right; it would have been better for the police to have been called straight away. It wasn't a big deal, believe me, Anna, and it would have been sorted by now. But instead Colette decided to get out of Berlin, just when the Fleischmanns were about to go to the police. Colette and me caught a night flight to London.'

'You did a runner!'

He smiled. 'Yes, I suppose we "did a runner". And now I feel bad, Colette feels bad, and we don't know when they might catch up with us. Yannis is still in Berlin. He's meant to be coming over, but I don't think that's going to happen. And as you know, it's all gone wrong here already.'

He waved an arm, indicating the room. Again she noticed the telescope at the window.

'This is a cell, isn't it?' he said. 'I'm being punished.'

He looked completely miserable, but she ignored it.

'You can see out. Tell me about the telescope, Wolf.'

'It's a good one.'

'I know,' said Anna. 'I've just had a go. Use it for looking into bedrooms, do you?'

Wolf looked horrified. 'What do you think I am, Anna?'

'I don't know, Wolf. Tell me.'

'I use it for looking at the hills, birds, the stars at night. And sometimes to watch people in the village doing stuff, but I'm not a...a...'

He stopped and stared at her, wanting her to believe him.

'But it's not a cell, this room,' she said. 'Not if you've done nothing wrong. You can leave any time you want, can't you?'

'But Colette – ' He stopped.

'So you're staying in here to keep your mother happy, are you? You're sixteen; tell her where to get off.'

He shrugged. He shrugged too much.

'You know what she's like, Anna.'

'Actually, Wolf, I think I understand algebra better than I understand Colette. I thought she was levelling with me *last* time. I thought we were friends. I obviously got that wrong.'

Hurt, Anna looked away, towards the computer.

'Wolf's Whin World get many hits, then?'

Wolf smiled ruefully. 'Not yet. It was Yannis's idea. You know, stuck in Whin but keep in touch with Berlin, New York, the rest of the world. They've found these learning packages for me, interesting websites. They always were anti-school, you know, all the competition, compulsory sport, all that, and now I don't go at all.'

'Lucky old Wolf!'

'You wouldn't think so if you were sitting up here all day, with a few books and a computer, and Colette coming in every hour to check I'm all right. You'd go stir-crazy.'

Anna remembered something. 'So to break the boredom you spy on sunbathers?'

Wolf looked caught out. 'Sorry, Anna. I wasn't spying. I just wanted to talk to someone. You.'

The door opened downstairs.

Colette called: 'Tea up! How's it going?'

She appeared up the steps, carrying a tray. She stopped, aghast.

'Anna!'

'Oh, hi! We were, er – '

Wolf cut in. 'We were talking about the college, the kind of courses I could do.'

OK, Wolf, if you say so.

'Yeah, they do all sorts, and there's no uniform or anything. You can smoke,' said Anna, doing the best she could. What the hell did she know about the college?

'No uniform? I should think not!' laughed Colette trying to be normal. 'But where do you...how did you – ?'

'She was out in the field,' lied Wolf. 'I shouted to her.'

'Oh right! Fine!' And Colette laughed again.

Go on, you might well blush, thought Anna. I'm not sure I can be bothered with you any more. My friend Colette.

Time to go.

'Anyway, Wolf's got assignments to do,' said Anna. 'I'm off. Catch you later.'

And though Colette was insisting she must stay, there was no problem, Anna squeezed past her, down the steps and out of the door.

20

Anna needed to talk to someone, but how could she tell anyone in Whin what she knew? Up in her bedroom she tore the middle out of a school exercise book and started writing.

Dear Dad,
Well you didn't miss much with the Bar-B-Cue. Nobody came really and the weather turned bad just for that day in honour. But Mum says youve got to hand it to Brian he organised it and did it off of his own bat. And he even made the Bar-B-Cue itself – it's still out the back now.

She paused, remembering the men in the toilet had predicted it. So, they were right. She also thought of the two days they had to eat left-over food, till she and the twins – together! – went on strike and the rest of it got thrown.

Oh and thanks for ringing. But I didn't want to tell you about the Bar-B-Cue it's boring. I think I told you about Colette in the village and her son Wolf who's in Berlin. Was! He's come to live in Whin and this is all a bit dodgy. He did something with a girl or should that be 'to a girl'? and even though Colette says it's all in the past well you don't know do you? But, Dad, I have met him I've just come from there and he seems a bit of a geek to be honest I mean to look at him you wouldn't think anything. Mind you how he survived living with those parents I don't know well I suppose he hasn't yet. PARENTS!!! I'm only telling you this because I haven't to tell anyone in the village and since it looks like you aren't coming over it doesn't matter but don't tell anyone anyway.

And you may have noticed we've been revising apostrophes at school, they're those little tadpole things you get when there's an s at the end of a word. So when you write back hint hint you'll be able to get your apostrophe's all correct let's hope.

Hugs and Kisses
Anna
(STILL YOUR DAUGHTER!!)

She wrote *apostrophe* in the margin and drew an arrow to an example of one. She went downstairs and got an envelope from her mother.

'It'd be great if he could be bothered to write back, Anna,' said her mother, 'but don't bet on it. He means well but he's bloody hopeless.'

She smiled ruefully at Anna.

'They're all the same that way, men. Though Brian did once write a poem for me in the early days, before we were going out properly.'

'A poem? Brian?'

'I've still got it upstairs.'

'Show us!'

'No way! You'd only take the mick.'

'Mum, would I do a thing like that? Does it rhyme and that?'

'Sort of.'

'There's no such thing as a sort-of-rhyme. So what's it about?'

'I told you, it was for me. It's about me.'

'Cath does another wash and set, that kind of thing.'

'It's got a refrain that goes: *Kathleen shine on me, like the moon on the sea*. Nice, isn't it?'

'God! How gross! And who's Kathleen?'

'Me. I told you it was early days. He thought my name was Kathleen instead of Catherine.'

'And this decided you to get off with him, Mum? Already he was confusing you with some other woman.'

Her mother laughed but went serious.

'Anna, send your dad your letter. Keep in touch because he won't. He loves you, in his own way, and when you're with him he'll spoil you rotten, but he'll let things slide – you'll have to do most of the work. And I'm sorry you and Brian don't get on better. He's a good person. He'll hang on in there, even if the going gets tough. I mean, look at that car.'

'I can't; it's in the garage. It's not going anywhere.'

Cath laughed again. 'OK, pet. I've no stamps. You'll have to get one from the shop.'

And as Anna took the 50p from her mother, she said: 'Lucky man, getting a letter from his daughter.'

She met Declan as she went out.

'Oh, thanks for that thing off the internet.'

90

'What?'

'You know, about Wolf. Thanks. He's been up there all the time.'

'What you on about?' he muttered and shook his head.

Anna stared at Declan for a moment, then walked off. You make an effort and just get grunted at. So why bother?

21

Now when Anna went up to Sneck Cottage, it was to the outhouse rather than the house. She didn't know if Colette was hurt, but serve her right. Whatever Colette's complicated reasons were, she hadn't been straight with Anna.

All the same, Colette found it difficult to leave Wolf and Anna alone. She was forever coming over to check that 'things were OK'.

One day after she'd stuck her head up into Wolf's room for the hundredth time, Wolf said, quietly bitter: 'It's all right, Colette, I haven't attacked her yet.'

Colette blinked, as if she'd been slapped.

'Wolf! Why are you saying that? I never thought… I'm only seeing if you want something, darling.'

'If we want anything, we'll get it.'

Her hurt look changed to one of suspicion, aimed at Anna. Was Anna giving her son lessons in being stroppy?

Colette opted for bright and breezy. 'In any case, I'm sure that Anna is quite capable of looking after herself, aren't you?'

As Colette shut the door behind her, Wolf grinned at Anna. He'd won a little victory. Thin face, wide smile, a good-looking screwball, who didn't seem to have any idea that he was good-looking. There was nothing look-at-me about his smile. He looked Anna straight in the eye.

And that was unusual these days. Boys and men – like Ron, the landlord in The Bull – looked her only briefly in the face before their eyes flicked down to her chest. The body that had been happily hers all her childhood now seemed to have been taken over by anybody who wanted to look over it. Flick, flick. But not Wolf. He looked her straight in the eye. If she forgot about his history, she felt safe with him. Safe with Wolf; strange!

Though he didn't walk round the village, Wolf's presence at Sneck Cottage was no longer a secret. Neither was the amount of time Anna spent up there.

Lydia as usual was on the case.

'Tell us about him, then, Anna.'

'Who're you talking about, Lydia?'

'Mister dark-and-mysterious up at Crockery Cottage.' A pan hissed as it boiled over. Lydia turned it off.

'Oh,' said Anna vaguely, 'I don't really know anything about him.'

'So you've stopped going up there?'

'He doesn't say much. Colette does the talking.'

'Aren't you the lucky one.'

'He's fed up with Berlin – he was getting bullied at school – so he's come here.' Anna listened to herself; so she was trying to get sympathy for Wolf, was she?

'Berlin! Listen to her! And he's got a daft name, they say.'

'You could say that. Wolf.'

Lydia grinned. 'Just wanted to hear you say it. Yes,

93

you're definitely interested!'

'Don't be pathetic!' But Anna could hardly say the reason was Wolf was on the run for child abuse.

'Anyroad, we can't spend all day talking about your love life. Go and put some plates to warm!'

Colette drove them over to Hebden Bridge to a craft fair, for the sake of somewhere to go. He blinked at the moors and big skies like an animal that had been kept in a hutch. He looked afraid of the world and desperate for it at one and the same time.

Another big adventure was to go to Boltby to get the college prospectus for Wolf to plan his future. Colette was going to give them a lift down but they convinced her they could manage the bus! Which was all right provided Wolf took his mobile and rang straight away if there was any problem and here's an emergency ten-pound note just in case and... God! Wolf, have you lived with this all your life?

They decided to stay to see an early evening film. Wolf rang and yes, that was all right and Colette would pick them up from the cinema afterwards and not to go off anywhere. They went to see the new Austin Powers film, and Wolf laughed like it was the funniest thing he'd ever seen. Probably it was. Two ordinary kids at the movies, eating popcorn – wow!

Soon Wolf risks walking through the village with Anna, to the shop, even to Anna's house. Luckily Brian's out of the way on a trip to a scrapyard looking for bits for the car – some wonderful must-visit graveyard of American cars somewhere in Scotland, and

Anna's mother knows how not to be embarrassing. Wolf even stays for tea and seems guilty about enjoying burger and chips from the freezer, as if it's some sort of wild extravagance. Burger and chips: welcome to the planet, Wolf.

Of course it isn't quite so simple, and later that evening Anna's mother uses the latest village news to sound a warning.

Rachel is pregnant, and nobody's surprised.

'Poor Rachel,' said Anna's mother. 'Just take notice, Anna.'

'What do you mean, take notice?' retorted Anna. 'Me and Wolf are just friends – do you think I'm stupid? You're all sex mad.'

'What you talking about?' asked Diarmid.

'Rachel's up the stick,' said Anna.

'What's that?' asked Declan.

Anna sighed. 'She's going to have a baby.'

'Yeugh!'

'Surely she's not going to have it!' said Anna's mother anxiously.

'Well, I don't know, do I? Not if she's got any sense, which she hasn't. Anyway, Mum, when did I ever need Rachel to teach me anything?'

'How can she not have it?' asked Declan.

'They sew you up so it can't get out,' said Anna.

'Do they?'

'Duur! You know nothing, thickos.'

'Well, you could help explain some basic things to them, instead of just making fun,' said her mother. 'I don't suppose Brian will have.'

'Do you think he knows them himself?'

'He knows more than you think,' her mother smiled at her.

'Don't, I'm going to be sick!' said Anna.

'Not morning sickness, is it?' said Diarmid.

'Hey! Cancel the facts of life lesson, Mum!' said Anna as Diarmid smirked. 'We've got a budding gynae-cologist here.'

'Anna!' said her mother sharply. 'It's you I'm think-ing about; don't do anything stupid.'

'OK, OK, OK.'

It was just too embarrassing to go on talking about it.

Lydia of course had a field day, trying to work out who was to blame – Rachel, Glenn, Glenn's father, Rachel's mother, young folk in general, television.

'Television?' said Anna.

'Well, it's all sex and swearing,' said Lydia.

'So it's the swearing that did it?'

'Don't get clever; you might live to regret it. That young fellow of yours, watch him!'

Anna stared at the mucky washing-up water and decided it wasn't worth arguing. Let them all think what they wanted, they would anyway.

22

Anna was watching TV with the twins when the two men from the council visited again. When Brian opened the door to them he obviously thought it was because of the car. His boss had told Brian to shift it out of the garage – he needed the space. 'Either it goes or you do, Brian old friend,' as Brian reported it, so yesterday it had been towed back to the house. It had a brick against the wheel to stop it rolling back because the brakes didn't work.

'Hey, it doesn't take you boys long!' Anna heard him say. 'Now let me guess which bloody snitch it was turned us in – the Phillipses again?'

'We're not here about the car, we didn't know it was back. But don't worry, Mr McManus, I'm sure you will be hearing from us about it.'

'So just a social visit, is it, boys?'

'We've received notice that these premises are being used for commercial purposes.'

'In English, please,' said Brian.

The other one said: 'You're using the house to carry on a business, a hairdresser's, which is in breach of tenancy rules.'

'Now wait a minute, as it happens my wife is out, but are you saying we can't do what we want in this house? It's us as pays the rent.'

'So you're saying there is a hairdressing business here?'

'I'm saying no such thing, and if you'll just excuse me – '

Brian stuck his head round the door and hissed at Anna, 'Get all that bloody hair stuff out of here!' waving an arm at the corner of the room where the ancient hairdryer stood, and slammed the door shut behind him. The arguing carried on at the front doorstep.

'Quick!' said Anna, unplugging the dryer. 'Take this out! Now!'

The twins moved faster than she'd ever seen, each taking an end and out through the kitchen. Anna grabbed brushes, tongs, scissors, bottles, threw them into a plastic carrier and stuck them in the broom cupboard. The mirror was screwed to the wall – it'd have to stay.

'If you don't believe me,' said Brian opening the door and silently questioning Anna with raised eyebrows, ' – see for yourselves.'

The council men shuffled in.

'See?' said Brian. 'Nothing.'

The older man picked up a sachet of hair dye from the coffee table and held it up accusingly.

'Yeah, hair dye,' said Anna nonchalantly. 'It's for hair. Probably every house in the universe has one. Except yours, of course.'

'Interesting place for a mirror,' said the younger man.

Anna said: 'That's why Brian put it there, didn't you? For interest. We have very boring lives.'

The older man was looking out of the back window,

pulling aside the net curtain. The hairdryer stood there, with the twins getting their breath back.

'Know anything about that, do we?' said the council man.

One of the twins put his head under the dryer. 'Beam me up, Scotty!' he shouted.

'Jesus!' said Brian. 'Now where did they find that?'

The council men had had enough.

'You'll be hearing from us, Mr McManus,' said the younger one, irritably, as they left.

'I'm sure I will,' said Brian, as he and Anna followed them out. 'You're not happy unless you're harassing innocent folk. It's like Nazi Germany!'

Mrs Phillips was in her garden.

'How can she get away with one of those?' Brian shouted after the council men, pointing to the stone boy. 'It's obscene! Time you boys paid her a visit. It's bloody pornographic!' And then, to Mrs Phillips' outraged face, 'Who would have thought it, such a beautiful woman with such a filthy mind. Tut tut.'

He winked at Anna as they went inside. He sang the refrain of an Irish freedom song, 'The Bold Fenian Men' – *O pay them back woe for woe,/Give them back blow for blow,/Out and make way for the bold Fenian men* – and cheered, the twins joining in. Not that they knew what Fenians were, or perhaps they did by now. Anna didn't ask.

When Anna's mother got back she said, 'Great victory, Brian, but what are we going to do? It's not a lot but the hairdressing pays for the extras. We're done for if they shut me down.'

'Quit moaning, woman, we're celebrating!'

He opened a can and poured some into a tumbler for her. She pulled a face but took it, and all five of them stood looking out of the back window at the hairdryer where it stood next to the Brian-B-Cue. It was like His and Hers, a weird chess queen and king ruling over the overgrown back garden of 7 Windermere Grove.

Anna's mother kissed Brian, then said: 'Best bring it in before it rains. Twins?' But they'd disappeared; life was back to normal.

The phone rang.

'*Anna?*'

'Dad.'

'*You OK?*'

'Yeah.'

'*You sound a bit, I don't know, down.*'

'It's nothing.'

'*Go on, what is it?*'

'If you want to know, it's you.'

'*Me? I'm all right.*'

'How would I know? I never see you.'

'*That's why I'm ringing, pet – what you doing next Saturday?*'

'You're coming over!'

'*Not quite – how do you fancy a day in Manchester?*'

'Dad, I would kill for a day in Manchester.'

'*Best put your mother on, then.*'

'Mum,' shouted Anna, 'can you speak to Dad? He wants me to meet him in Manchester.'

'Not on your own,' she said coming to the phone.

'You know how reliable he is. Michael? What's all this, then?'

Anna listened to her mother's half of the conversation with a sinking heart, then suddenly she had an idea.

'Wolf!'

'Sorry, Anna?' said her mother.

'Suppose Wolf comes with me – ask Dad if that's all right?'

'There'd be two of you, I suppose it'd be all right,' mused her mother.

'Dad,' said Anna grabbing the phone, 'can Wolf come?'

'*Isn't he the lad who –* '

'Yeah, he's older than me. We'll be fine.'

'*OK with me, kid.*'

The pips started going.

'*I'm out of change, pet. Where we meeting then?*'

'Er, front of the Town Hall.'

'*Right. High noon?*'

'What?'

'*12 o'clock.*'

'Ring before Saturday and I'll tell you if Wolf's OK to come – '

Brrrrrrrrr.

Of course he didn't ring, but it didn't matter. Colette okayed it for Wolf to go; he'd survived Boltby so he could move on to the next challenge. She insisted Wolf call and see his friend Lucien, son of an architect friend, while they were in Manchester.

Wolf said to Anna, 'Lucien's a complete messer.'

She smiled: 'messer'. It was a word he'd got off her.

'He's older than me and we never liked each other but Colette wants to believe Lucien and me are real good buddies. You'll see for yourself, when we call and see him.'

23

Manchester city centre. A place Anna thought she knew but she'd forgotten how tall the buildings were, how narrow that made the streets feel, how fast it pushed the crowds along, so that even though she and Wolf were early and had time to stroll, they found they weren't strolling but having to go as fast as everyone else. Those incredible people in their million-dollar clothes and hair styles you didn't believe existed outside of magazines, women with their long legs and disdainful faces, and who didn't even look at Anna and Wolf. Hey, this is my city too, Anna felt like saying, I'm no hick from the sticks. Except she knew she was now.

The city entered her veins, a hit that had been here all the time – while she'd been sitting on a wall not fifty miles away, listening to sheep bleating! Good to be back.

With an hour to kill before they met her dad, Anna could show off where she knew. But a couple of turnings she got wrong, and she'd forgotten how far it was, so they got to the Town Hall bang on 12 o'clock.

Her dad wasn't there.

They walked right round the Town Hall and back to the front, just to make sure he wasn't at some other entrance. They sat on the monument and waited, chatting.

By half past he hadn't showed. Anna could tell Wolf

103

was making a real effort to keep her spirits up. The hit of being in the city was wearing off.

By quarter to they'd starting talking about what they would do. There was nothing to panic about. They had money. There were buses home. And if you think, you stupid, stupid whatever you are that I'm not going to enjoy myself just because you're too stupid to get your act together and turn up to meet your daughter, and if you think I'd even think of crying because you're too stupid to ... to ...

After watching her cry for a while Wolf hesitantly put an arm round her shoulders.

'I'm OK,' she sniffed, but kept on crying. She was aware of the awkward little pats his hand was making, not really knowing what to do.

'Oh, Wolf, where – why didn't he – ?'

She buried her face in his shoulder. Slowly, she stopped crying and became aware of how uncomfortable his collarbone was. Her crying had put smudgy eyeliner marks on his shirt.

'Sorry about that.'

'It's OK. My pleasure,' said Wolf smiling ruefully.

'Well, sod it!' said Anna, standing up. 'Sod him! We're here now, let's go for it.'

'All right, but can we just do Lucien first? I promised I would ...' his voice trailing away. Colette bossing him around still.

'God, Wolf! We're in the greatest city on earth, and you want us to spend the afternoon with some dork because your mother thinks it's good for you.'

'It won't take long, it's only Cheetham Hill.'

'What buses go up there?'

'Buses? We'll get a cab.'

Of course, Colette had given Wolf what looked like a fair stack of money.

'Good old Colette! Right, I'll give it an hour, then back to do the shops, is it a deal?'

So Wolf got on his mobile to let Lucien know they were on their way.

The house was amazing. Anna stared at it while Wolf paid the cab driver.

'Are you sure this is it?'

''Course I am. We stayed here when Colette was looking for somewhere to buy.'

It was modern and huge; the roofs stacked up as if they didn't quite match.

'Lucien's father's an architect, designed it himself. Actually he says "built it himself", but he doesn't mean that.'

The middle part of the house, where the door was, was all glass – you could see right through to the garden out the back. Wolf rang the bell which was set in the middle of a woman's face whose hair was all writhing snakes. Weird. Nothing happened for ages, then Anna saw this boy a bit older and taller than Wolf approaching the door. He was carrying something, and as he opened the door to them she saw it was a kitten.

'Hi, Wolfie!' he said in a rich, confident voice. 'How're you doing?'

'Hello, Lucien. Fine. This is Anna. My friend.'

'Hi, friend Anna. Have a kitten!' And he handed her the white kitten that looked only days old. It made funny little mewing noises. 'It's a pedigree in case you're wondering – a Persian, worth a few hundred quid, but you can have it for free. On the house. Come on in!'

And he walked off across the wooden floor of the entrance lobby, bigger than the village hall dance floor, without bothering to see if they were following.

'Amazing house,' whispered Wolf, 'I'll show you round.'

'The folks are away,' said Lucien over his shoulder. 'Some sort of conference in Japan or somewhere. I could have gone, but – bor-ing!'

Anna was hardly listening. Lucien had led them into the kitchen, at least Anna assumed it was the kitchen. The cooker was in the middle of the room with all these steel and copper utensils hanging from a rack above it. God knows what they were all for; it could have been a torturer's kit. And above it, going up to the high ceiling, a huge copper hood for fumes.

'I was just going to make lunch – you haven't eaten yet, have you?' Lucien asked, staring at Anna. Casually, taking his time, he looked her over, up and down.

Anna shook her head.

'Anna,' said Lucien, putting his hands on his hips, mock-seriously, 'house rules are: those who don't speak, don't get. So we'll try that again, shall we? Would you like some lunch, Anna?'

'Thank you, Lucien, lunch would be delightful!' said

Anna brightly. We can all play silly buggers.

'That's better. Rule number two: no cats in the kitchen.'

Anna had forgotten about the kitten. It was heaving itself around her cupped hands pathetically and mewing. What was she meant to do with it?

'Its mother's in the greenhouse, Wolfie; show her where that is. Meanwhile, your chef will produce a culinary delight in a matter of moments.' He bowed low to them.

'Oh, and Anna,' said Lucien moving in a bit closer, 'I think you might want to give that eye make-up a little attention; it's a complete mess!'

Wolf led Anna to the greenhouse.

'Is Lucien like that all the time?' asked Anna.

'Try living with him for a week.'

'I'll pass on that.'

But being here was like nothing else. The lawn they were crossing to the greenhouse was cropped as close as the pool table in The Bull; it gave Anna's steps a spring. It was like walking on air. Time out, Anna, enjoy it.

The mother cat was a fluffy white spiteful-looking thing that hissed at them. Anna dropped the kitten among its equally revolting brothers and sisters, all crawling around in a helpless way.

'Come on,' said Wolf, 'I'll show you round.'

But the house was so huge even Wolf went wrong. Each room had its own special design, corners weren't square, ceilings weren't flat, light coming in from above, or below, or a whole wall of glass. Walls and floors were bare, except for beautiful rugs in the middle of vast pale wood floors or hung on white walls. Every now and again there'd be a painting, a huge vase or a carving. The Brian-B-Cue would look great in here as a modern sculpture, thought Anna.

In the largest room there were two long and low settees, pure white, facing each other across the room. Anna sat on one and told Wolf to sit on the other. It was like looking the length of a football pitch at the other goalposts.

'So do Mr and Mrs Lucien Bollockchops sit in here at night and watch "Coronation Street"?' asked Anna.

'Search me,' said Wolf.

'That's a point, where's the telly?'

'There's a special TV room – one whole wall is the screen. Didn't I show it you?'

'You'll have to speak up, I can't hear this far away. Do they use mobiles to ring from one settee to the other, do you think?'

'I said there's a special TV room – '

'OK, Wolf, only joking.'

Anna thought of the living room at 7 Windermere Grove. They'd got a new three piece suite when they moved in. It had filled the room – there was no space for anything else, or to walk even – and they'd had to put one of the chairs upstairs to make way for the hairdressing chair.

Someone shouted somewhere, very faintly.

'That's Lucien. Lunch, I believe, is served.' And Wolf raised his eyebrows and smiled. 'Come on.'

24

Well, it wasn't shopping in the city-centre stores, but perhaps this wasn't too bad. And Lucien was all right when you got used to him, in fact he was funny in an upper-class twit sort of way. He was eighteenish and obviously no one ever told him where to get off.

He'd set the table in the kitchen and opened the patio doors so you could hear the birds singing in the garden. Was this really Manchester? White tablecloth, flowers in the centre, and each of the three place settings had a tall wine glass and a napkin in a silver ring. Every little thing was different and interesting and classy – and way over the top. Even the knives looked as if they'd been designed by rocket scientists. All this for a bit of dinner. Lunch. It should have been McDonald's, or perhaps her dad would have taken them somewhere a bit posher.

But cancel that thought; best not even think about him.

Lucien put bread on the table, French bread of course, and presumably that's a French bread-board it's on, all dark and medieval looking. Medieval bugs on it too, by the look of it.

'It's only an omelette. All right I hope? I was cooking for friends last night so I'm a bit pissed off with the old haute cuisine.'

'Whatever, Lucien, whatever,' said Wolf.

'Provided it's not mushroom,' said Anna.

'Oh, and what have mushrooms ever done to you?'

'I can't stand the feel of them, the – what's the word?'

'Texture?'

'Yeah. They're like fried slug.'

'Ah, now, in some countries it's a great delicacy, fried slug.'

'Don't, Lucien, I'll throw up,' she said.

'Anyway, rest easy, my dear Anna – it's not mushroom but humble *fromage*.'

'Oh, ham's all right.' I know what *fromage* is, you clever arse; let's see how stupid you think I am.

He gave her a sideways look, unsure. Trying it on, Anna Whoever-you-are?

'Salad,' he announced, putting a large hand-painted bowl full of greenery on the table. 'No slugs in there, Anna. I don't think.'

'That's one of Colette's,' she exclaimed, 'that bowl.'

'Is it?'

''Course it is, it's her style.'

'Well, you're probably right,' drawled Lucien.

'Wolf. Is it or isn't it?'

'It looks like it,' ventured Wolf.

Was he afraid of contradicting his friend?

'Oh, forget it,' said Anna, irritated that neither of them seemed very interested.

'Suit yourself,' said Lucien. He tipped the beaten egg into the frying pan – a cloud of smoke and steam sizzling up into the copper hood.

'What do we want to drink, then? Red or white? Wolf, your shout.'

'I'm not bothered about wine,' said Wolf.

'House rule number 57: good wine is always served here. Anna?'

'Food's all I want, I'm starving.'

'OK, I'll pick something. Eeny, meeny...' He pulled a bottle of wine out of the rack. 'We seem to be on Côtes du Rhône, everybody. Open it, Wolfie.' He lobbed it over to Wolf, who only just managed to catch it, then grabbed the omelette pan, shook it, folded the omelette in half and slid in onto a plate.

'There we go – who's first? Anna?'

Was she supposed to clap this performance.

But it tasted good, she had to admit that, and when all three of them were sitting down eating omelette and even the salad managed to taste interesting and Lucien had poured out red wine for all three even though they'd said no, Anna felt good. She even picked up her wine glass and swished it round. It looked brilliant, but the taste! Totally unsweet even if it looked like Ribena and so bitter it sucked your cheeks in, but it was a different world so different rules applied. She drank most of it but stopped when Lucien filled her glass again.

Then there was pudding – 'a few profiteroles left over from last night' – which were pastry ball things, all cream and chocolate, and some mouldy blue cheese nobody touched but it looked good. Lucien put on some music, something classical on strings that came out of invisible speakers. Classical music, in the kitchen!

So people really lived like this – and here she was, living it too. For an hour.

'Everybody happy?' asked Lucien lazily, confident no one would say no.

'Cool!' said Anna. Except that it was Saturday afternoon and they were in Manchester. Time to stop playing with the toffs. 'But we need to go – I'm meeting my dad. Father.'

Wolf looked surprised but said nothing.

'New house rule,' said Lucien. 'Everybody has to see the new summerhouse. It's Mummy's new *folie de grandeur* – she thinks it's Versailles.'

Anna didn't have a clue what he was on about and she'd had enough.

'We need to go,' said Wolf, picking up on Anna's mood.

'It'll take two minutes,' said Lucien. 'Put the stuff in the dishwasher, Wolf, earn your keep. Come on, Anna.' He put an arm round her to steer her into the garden. She glanced back at Wolf, who shrugged and started picking up dirty dishes. Difficult to say no to Lucien.

'Ever been to Versailles?' he asked Anna. Obviously she hadn't so he could tell her all about it as they walked across the long lawn, making it sound incredibly impressive and terribly boring at the same time. He'd dropped his arm; she felt better about that.

The summerhouse was built on a little hill with steps up to it. The front half was glass and had wicker furniture in it; there was a wicker settee on ropes like a swing.

'Go on, Anna, give it a try. You're not too old.'

She climbed on to it and pushed it into motion.

'And in the back there we have a toilet for those who can't make it to the house.' He made fun of it all, and loved it at the same time. He was just a spoilt brat.

He sat down next to Anna, the ropes creaking with the extra weight.

'You didn't sort out that eyeliner, as I asked,' he said, peering closely at her face. She could smell the food and wine on his breath.

'Anyway, Anna, what's an attractive girl like you doing with a loser like Wolf?'

Uh-oh. I don't know where he wants this to go, but I'm not going there.

'Shove off, Lucien.'

'Not the nicest thing to say to a guy who's made you so welcome.' And he put one hand behind her head and started to kiss her.

Think, Anna. Is this what rich kids expect for making your dinner and letting you see their poncy fucking houses? Breath like a garbage can and a tongue half way down your throat. But this is one big guy, so do you upset him? You can't push him over like Wolf. By the way, Wolf, where are you?

He lifted his face off hers.

'I think we're a bit interested, aren't we?'

'I think not, Lucien. You can stop right now.'

But now he had a hand on her leg and he kissed her again. She tried to move his hand but she couldn't budge it.

She pulled away from his stinking mouth and yelled.

'Wolf!'

'He'll be busy stacking the dishwasher and keeping out of the way, like a good little Wolfie. Unless you want him to join in too – I wouldn't have thought you were so, um, advanced at your age.'

'Wolf!'

He started kissing her again and his hand was up her skirt. He wasn't a sophisticated host any more but someone who didn't care about anything or anybody, certainly not her.

She had to fight.

Over his shoulder a face appeared at the glass door: Wolf climbing the steps. He stopped and stared – then turned and went back down the steps and disappeared. Bastard! So he was in on this. It was some big set-up with his old friend Lucien. Who was now tugging at her knickers.

She was on her own.

She pushed her hand hard into his face, one finger going right up his nostril to where it was slimy.

He jerked his head back and swore, grabbing her arm and twisting it behind her. She bit his ear hard. It was like getting a piece of gristle in a meat pie.

He stood up, and smiled a Hugh Grant smile.

'If I weren't a perfect gentleman, I wouldn't let you get away with this. But the question is: am I a perfect – ?'

He didn't finish. Wolf appeared in the door behind him, in his hands a garden spade. As Lucien half turned towards him, Wolf lifted the spade and swung it down. It didn't hit him properly and glanced off his expensive haircut, but it was enough. For a surprised moment Lucien hesitated between Wolf and Anna, like someone not knowing who to go for in a game of tig. Before he'd made his mind up, Anna was off the settee swing and out of the door. Wolf dropped the spade and ran too.

Lucien didn't run after them. They could hear him shouting after them.

'Nice entertaining you, Anna; please stay a little longer next time. And as for you, Wolfie, I think you know what's good for you. 'Bye, chaps!'

25

No cabs. They dived on the first bus.

'So much for your friend Lucien!' said Anna, as they sat down, top deck. She hitched her skirt up to see where his nails had scratched her leg. 'Look at that! The bastard.'

'I never thought he was like that, Anna. He was always playing the bored aristocrat – '

'You could have fooled me!'

'But I never imagined he'd try it on like that. Do you think he was drunk?'

'Oh thanks, Wolf, let's start making excuses for rapists!'

He smiled apologetically and said nothing. Down below walking along the pavement were two Jewish men in black hats and coats with long dangly sideburns. They looked hot.

'For a minute, Wolf, I thought you were in on it.'

'What, with Lucien?'

'You appeared, then vanished. I thought there was a plan.'

'Thanks, Anna.' He stared at the graffiti on the seat back with a dark, bitter stare.

He said: 'I can't ever *really* convince you, can I?'

'Hey, Wolf,' and it felt funny, trying to cheer him up after what had just happened, 'it was only for a moment.

And you can't blame me for thinking it, can you? I mean, there you were, then gone!'

'I suppose not.'

'And then you came riding to the rescue, spear, white horse, all that.'

'I wanted to kill him,' said Wolf darkly. 'I wanted to smash his stupid head in.'

'Well, thanks, Wolf, but he was only some overgrown kid trying it on. And he was beginning to see sense!' She tried to lighten it. All too close to home for Wolf?

'I wanted to kill him.'

'Pick a better weapon next time, then.' She giggled at her image of Wolf trying to swing the spade that looked too big for him and the way it flattened Lucien's expensive haircut. 'Wasn't there a garden fork? Ugh! Right through his guts.'

'There was only a garden roller.'

'That would do. Here, Lucien, put your bollocks under this!'

Finally Wolf managed to laugh.

They could smell the brewery as they approached the town centre.

'What did he mean, that last thing he shouted, about you knowing what's good for you? Does he know something?' asked Anna.

'I suppose,' said Wolf slowly, 'he might know about the Steffi thing. He's clever and he's devious. But I don't think he'll say anything, unless we do.'

'No, I suppose not.'

So that was the end of it. Goodbye, Lucien.

Manchester centre again, but the magic had gone out of it. Was it worth staying, or should they just get the next bus home? Even the strangers on the streets seemed to stride less purposefully than before.

'What do you want to do, Wolf?'

'It's your day, Anna, I don't really...'

'Hey, it's Dad!'

And there he was, down there on the pavement, shirt and jeans, walking his confident walk.

'Dad! Dad!' She banged on the window. Yes, it was him! But though he heard something and looked round, he didn't look up.

'Come on, quick!' She ran along the aisle and down the stairs.

'We've got to get off!' she demanded of the lady driver.

She gave Anna a cool look.

'Next stop, the bus station, angel.'

'But it's my dad, I've got to talk to him.'

The bus stopped at some lights.

'OK,' said the driver, opening the door. 'There you go. And I know nothing about it.'

They were off and running back along the street. There he was – sun shining on him and smiling.

'Hey, Anna, what you doing here?' He was pleased and puzzled at the same time.

She hugged him hard.

'Oh, Dad, where were you?'

'When?'

'12 o'clock, Town Hall, Saturday. Remember?'

'12 o'clock, Town Hall, *next* Saturday.'

'This is next Saturday.'

'No it's not, it's this Saturday. Next Saturday is next Saturday.'

'Dad, you're blooming hopeless.'

'It's a funny thing, Anna, that's what they all say. But I think you'll find I'm right this time.'

'I don't care. Anyhow, say hello to Wolf.'

'Hi, Wolf. She's a smasher, isn't she? And I'll tell you what, Anna, I wouldn't have known you. You've grown, kid.' And he looked her up and down.

'Yeah, well, we'll skip that. And it wouldn't be such a shock if you saw me more often.' What the hell, this is today, here, now. 'So what're we doing?'

'Well, the thing is, because it's not next Saturday – '

'OK, OK.'

'– it's a bit, like, complicated.'

'Why?'

'I'm meeting someone.'

Anna knew he meant a girlfriend.

'So what's the problem? Doesn't she know about me?'

'She doesn't know about anything yet.'

'It's time to find out then. When are you meeting her?' demanded Anna. She wasn't going to back off now.

'Off the next Salford bus,' he said, checking his watch.

'Fine. Let's go meet it.'

At the bus station their bus driver was carrying the cash box into the office. She winked at Anna.

'You got him then, your dad? Worth breaking company regulations for!' She smiled at him; he smiled back.

'Dad! You're the most disgusting flirt,' said Anna, pleased.

Deborah, her father's new girlfriend, was pretty but older than him and too well dressed to be getting off the Salford bus on a Saturday afternoon. She hardly batted an eyelid when she saw the three of them waiting for her.

'Hello, Michael,' she said, kissing him lightly. 'Brought along some friends, have you?'

When Anna and Wolf were introduced she took it all in her stride.

'Shops for an hour – what do you say, Anna? And then a film and something to eat. OK, everybody?'

And if spoiling the daughter was buying her way to her father's heart, well, that was fine with Anna. It had been a hard day, she was ready for something easy.

So they did sexy underwear in Kendals while her dad and Wolf hung around and tried to make conversation, joined the crush to see the early evening showing of the latest James Bond, rang home to get permission to sleep over at her dad's because it was getting late, and wound up in an Italian restaurant where the waiter flirted blatantly with both Deborah and Anna.

In the restaurant Anna's dad drank far too much and said how much he loved Anna, and how much he loved Anna's mother, and how it had been his fault it had ended, and how much you should look after someone who loved you and not throw it away, and how much he loved Deborah, and…But Deborah stopped him right there.

'Yes, Michael, and I love you too.' She kissed him again, in the same, brisk, light way. 'I think they're waiting to shut.'

Their waiter was now standing with an older waiter at the back of the restaurant, yawning. It had all been part of the service.

They caught a cab back to her dad's flat. He had forgotten all about sleeping on the settee and almost as soon as they were in he was steering Deborah into the one bedroom. She came out with a quilt and a couple of pillows, and Wolf and Anna pulled the settee cushions onto the floor to make up a bed. They didn't speak.

They lay on the cushions, still dressed. Then Anna reached across and took Wolf's hand and they lay in silence until they had to start talking to cover up the embarrassing sounds from the bedroom. It had been a long time since they had set off from Whin and too much had happened, so they talked about the film and laughed at bits again. The noises from the bedroom soon stopped.

Suddenly Anna said, 'D'you want to do it?'

'What?'

'I asked if you wanted, you know, to do it.'

A strange day already, and here she was making it stranger. She'd flipped!

Wolf hesitated, then said: 'You don't have to. It's all right.'

'I know I don't have to. I asked you.'

'Anna; things are complicated enough.'

'OK. I wouldn't want to be another complication.'

'I didn't mean that.'

'You did. But it's OK.'

After another pause, Wolf said: 'If you really think it would help – '

Anna laughed. 'Help? No, I'm sure you're right; it would be a complication.'

Actually 'complicated' didn't begin to describe the different feelings colliding with each other in her head right now, including not knowing why she'd asked him in the first place, but relief won out over disappointment.

Then she said: 'Here.'

She put his hand on her leg where Lucien had hurt it, and said in a baby voice: 'Rub it better!'

And with Wolf's timid paw resting on her leg, lying on the lumpy cushions, with far too much to think about, she went to sleep.

In the middle of the night she half woke and thought that all round the world there were people lying in beds, some with another person, some on their own, and that was OK.

This seemed the most profound idea to her. She pictured the dark spinning ball of the planet with all these little horizontal people asleep. But then she thought only half of it would be dark, the other half would be day, and those people wouldn't be asleep, and it all got too confusing, and she went back to sleep.

26

Wolf was asleep, his mouth slightly open.

Anna stood up and went to the kitchen for a drink of water. Her clothes were all creased and she wanted a shower. It was early and the light was grey. She shivered; there was a chill, as if overnight summer had ended.

Deborah came in, looking for the kettle. She was wearing one of Anna's dad's cotton shirts.

'Morning, love.' She yawned and stretched. 'Someone ought to invest in a new mattress. Not that someone's got any trouble sleeping on it; he's dead to the world.'

She gave Anna a longer look.

'Everything all right?'

'Yeah. I just need to get home.'

'I feel exactly the same. Boyfriends are all right but you can't beat a good bath. Is he your boyfriend, that Wolf?'

'I don't know. Probably.'

'Ah well, in your own time. He seems a nice kid.'

'Suppose so.'

Deborah came closer. Her eyes were friendly but worried, her skin a bit puffy, and Anna could see a faint fuzz of downy hair on her cheek against the morning light. For a crazy moment Anna wanted to take the older woman's face in her hands and reassure her, she didn't know how, perhaps only by telling her about all the electrolysis and tweezering and waxing her mother did. But Deborah would have known all about that. The moment passed.

'Enjoy yourself, Anna. It's a tough world and it gets tougher. If you can have a laugh, then have it. He's all right, your dad, a bit of a laugh, but he doesn't really care about me. He does care about you, though.'

She laughed, mocking herself.

'Listen to me going on. I'm sorry, Anna, I don't know how to talk to kids. I never had any, never will, not now. Lucky Michael to have a daughter like you. Lucky Anna's mother.'

The nearer Anna got to the adult world the sadder and more screwed up it seemed.

Deborah took two mugs of coffee back into the bedroom, and Anna went and stood in the doorway of the kitchen, looking at Wolf asleep on the cushions.

27

The police were up at Sneck Cottage within the week. They'd found out about Wolf and Steffi.

He rang Anna.

'It was Lucien, it must have been,' he said. 'They didn't give his name of course; "acting on information received" is the way they put it.'

'So the police act just because a spoilt kid like Lucien grasses you up?'

'I don't know. Perhaps he rang Steffi's parents; maybe the German police are involved.'

'So why did he do it?'

But Anna knew the answer; anything to get back at her, at Wolf, anything for a bit of a laugh. Lucien didn't care about anyone.

'We could report him,' said Anna. 'You know, for the summerhouse.'

'That's up to you, Anna. But think about it. The police won't just say: OK, we'll take your word. They'll grill you, and me, and him, for days, I expect, and before it even gets to court. And then they'll do it all again, in public, and Lucien's folk will have the best lawyers and barristers they can get. Think about it.'

'But it's just not fair!'

'You know what they'll do? They'll say we're making

125

it up, to get him back for reporting me. Otherwise, why didn't we go straight to the police in the first place? You and me, we're friends, aren't we? It's the kind of thing you do to help a friend, make something up like that.'

Anna was silenced. He was right, there wasn't anything they could do.

'So what are they going to do, Wolf, the police?'

'They don't know yet. We've been down to the police station. They're "making inquiries into a certain incident that occurred in Berlin six months ago concerning Steffi Fleischman". Obviously the Fleischmanns have complained, so they have to investigate.'

'Do you miss her?' Anna asked.

'Who?'

'Steffi.'

'I hope she's OK, but no, I wouldn't say I miss her.' He paused. 'Did I ever tell you she looks a bit like you?'

'No.'

'Well, it's only looks. Skin deep, they say.'

'Wolf, I'm not Steffi, I'm Anna. Got that?'

'Hey, what's the problem?'

Was he as innocent as he sounded or playing mind games? She couldn't tell.

'Why did you say she looks like me, if it's only skin deep?'

'It's not important.'

'Not to you, Wolf.' But she was starting to sound silly, making a big deal out of nothing.

'OK.'

'At least you don't look like anybody. Luckily for them.'

'Sorry, Anna.'

'I'm sorry, Wolf – it's you who's having the hard time. What do Colette and Yannis say?'

'They're scared stiff there's going to be some sort of trial, but I think they're glad it's all out in the open.'

'In the open? There's only me in Whin knows anything about it. Jimmy Tat'll be on the case, though. You know that, don't you?'

'Why should the village postman know anything?'

'He just does. X-ray eyes. But I won't say anything.'

'Thanks. See you later?'

'Yeah, I'll come up after tea.'

And as she hung up Anna realised she'd gone from wanting to get the truth out into the open, to wanting to keep it covered; from saying everything to saying nothing.

Colette met Anna at the door. She was very cool.

'Oh, hi, Anna. It's not very convenient right now.'

'You mean he's not allowed to play out?'

'No need to be sarcastic, Anna, but since you put it like that . . . I think you know what's happened.'

'Yeah, Wolf rang me. He said to come up, but if he's not allowed . . .'

'Oh, you'd better come in.'

'If it's not convenient . . .'

'It's just we don't want to make things more fraught, right now. I'm sure you understand.'

Suddenly Anna realised what she was talking about; it wasn't the police investigation, it was Anna and Wolf. To be exact, it was what her talented son was doing messing with some village loser like Anna. She felt a surge of anger.

Colette said: 'It's a difficult time, Anna, for everyone.'

'Dead right. Does that include me?'

'I'm sure it does.'

'Are you? Are you really?' There was no stopping Anna now. 'I'm fourteen, going nowhere, stuck in Whin, lousy Saturday job. And then you move here, want me to be friends with your dodgy son. So that's all right, no sweat, even if it means nearly being raped by some rich tosser friend of the family...'

'What are you talking about, Anna, what's this?'

'It doesn't matter, does it, because all that matters in the end is Colette and her precious son.'

'Tell me, Anna – is this something to do with Lucien?'

'Forget it, Colette.' She was near to tears, and she wasn't going to let Colette see her cry. 'You make me sick. Tell Wolf...I came up...'

She turned and ran.

28

Anna had had enough. She'd sooner be down in her tatty council house, even with snotty neighbours, even with Brian and the twins, than up at Sneck Cottage. It had been great to start with: learning to throw pots, the simple magic of it, it had been an escape, but it had turned into something too complicated. She didn't know what anyone wanted; she didn't know what she wanted. Well, Wolf could get in touch – he knew her number.

Meanwhile summer was over, like really; it was school again. It was a shock to walk back into the same school smell; nothing had changed. They tried of course – you're on GCSEs now, it's important you do well, it'll decide what you do next, etc. etc. – but they couldn't make Anna feel like it mattered.

Wolf was going to the college, to do art. At least, that's what they'd talked about before; Wolf was very artistic, of course.

The twins had finished at the village primary school. She'd totally forgotten until the last night of the holiday and the sorting out of the uniforms. They would be getting on the same bus as her in the morning, to come to her school.

'If you see me, just don't speak to me, right?' Anna ordered them. 'I don't know you.'

'Anna!' said her mother sharply. 'It's not easy for them. Do the big sister, can't you?'

'I had to do it for myself, no big sister for me. Not that I'm a sister, can I remind you?'

'Well, thanks for making the effort, Anna.' Doing sarcastic made her mother nervous; it didn't come naturally.

'It's OK,' said Declan, in his too-big, cheap, second-hand blazer, 'we don't need her.'

'Fine by me,' said Anna.

'You'll be OK, boys,' said Anna's mother, putting on a bright smile for them. 'At least you've got each other.'

'As always,' said Anna. 'The gruesome twosome.' And she went upstairs to see if there was any homework she should have done.

There was. She was meant to have read the first two chapters of a book. It was called *To Kill a Mockingbird*. It'd take ages. She checked; 28 pages, and there were 287 pages in the whole book. She took it to her bed, reading the blurb on the back to get the idea.

There was a knock on the door.

'Yeah?'

It was Declan. He came in and just stood.

'Declan, I've got to read this. Tonight.'

He didn't answer. What was he after?

'If you don't mind,' said Anna.

Then he said quietly, 'I'm not Declan. I'm Diarmid.'

She laughed, nervously. 'Yeah; of course.'

'You don't always get it wrong, but sometimes you do. When you bother to speak. I keep waiting for you to say thanks for the thing I got off the internet for you. But no.'

'But I thought it was Declan...'

And that just proved his point. She couldn't be bothered to tell them apart. This was awful.

'Why do you hate me? Both of us?'

'I don't hate you. Don't be ridiculous!'

'Mostly you ignore us. And Dad. Or else you're nasty. What have we done to you?'

She had to think who he meant by 'dad'. Brian of course.

'But Diarmid, what do you mean?'

'It's not our fault. That we're all living together. Isn't it all right?'

'Only when you spend all day on computer games!' She tried to make a joke.

'We don't spend all day playing computer games. Just because we used to do it a lot, you think we still do. You don't know what we do. You don't care.'

Anna was speechless.

'Dad's getting fed up. I heard him shouting at your mum the other night. About you. I couldn't really hear what he said, but... You know something, when he said you were coming to live, at the start, he said, "Wait till you meet, Anna, boys, she's something else!" He liked you. He used to like you.'

Anna's mother shouted up for him. Without any expression on his face, he turned and walked out. Anna had never stared as hard at Diarmid. She would get him right next time.

She tried to read the book.

When he was nearly thirteen, my brother Jem got his arm badly broken at the elbow. When it healed, and Jem's fears of never being able to play football were assuaged –

What's that mean: 'assuaged'? Oh, hell, buggering hell, buggering buggering hell!

29

A letter from Colette, by post – all the way from Sneck Cottage! People are weird. Lovely cream paper though, and really stylish handwriting.

Dear Anna,

This may seem rather a roundabout way to contact you but I am finding it difficult to talk to anyone just now, apart from necessary communication with the police. Normally I would escape to the wheel and throw a pot to help me relax but I'm so out of sorts that doesn't work either, which aggravates the whole situation.

I want to apologise for the other night. You were right. I thought long and hard afterwards about what you said and you were right; I can't have you as a friend for Wolf on my *terms. You must be with each other as you would wish to be. You are never less than welcome up at Sneck Cottage; I can't say it more plainly.*

The second thing is Lucien. I spoke at length to Wolf about it and think I have a good idea what happened. Again, all I can do is apologise; it is largely my fault you were placed in a very unpleasant situation and one that could have been even worse. I have spoken to Lucien's parents –

Oh God, Colette, keep out, keep out!

– and found them rather less than helpful. They wondered if Wolf's account could be relied upon as being quite accurate. I thought they might have been rather more sympathetic. At any rate, they are speaking to Lucien about it, but I rather think it is up to you whether you pursue it. If you choose to you have my full support.

Thank you for nothing, Colette, but even if Lucien were in the dock and I could get him locked up, I wouldn't go near him. Talk about turning a scary moment into a big production number.

The other question I raised with them was whether Lucien was likely to have reported Wolf to the police. They were quite adamant that Lucien would do no such thing, so we can only speculate.

However the police found out, find out they did, and we shall have to wait and see if they decide to take it further. If that should happen I can't begin to think what it will mean for Wolf, and for us, or for you of course. Well, we shall see.

Come up soon. I hope *you can think of this as another home.*

Your friend, Colette

It was funny how Colette didn't have a clue, even if she was making an effort. After school Anna went up to Sneck Cottage and chatted to them both, going into full airhead mode to try and cheer them up. It usually worked, but right now it was too much of an effort for

134

all three of them. Wolf sat expressionless and said nothing for the hour she was there. There was nothing to be done but suffer till it was over.

Colette came to the door and hugged her.

'Thanks, Anna,' and she smiled grimly.

30

Too much had happened already that summer, and now the police were onto Wolf. Six months ago she'd been sitting on the wall with Rachel, bored out of her skull; she could have done with a piece of that now. Six months ago as an avid reader of *J17* she could have put it all in a letter to the Problem Page.

Dear J17, The council keep giving us a hard time but we beat them hands down every time so that's not a problem. I hated my mother's boyfriend and his kids but I understand them all better now so that's not a problem. My boyfriend had underage sex with someone but he's probably going to get done so that's not a problem. And he isn't really my boyfriend so even less of a problem. I haven't seen much of my dad but recently we had a day out together so that's not a problem. Anna.

Dear Anna, So what is your problem? J17.

Well, how the hell was she supposed to know? It was her age, it was the world, it was Wolf, it was Colette... Anyway, she'd stopped reading *J17*, it was for kids.

At least one thing was certain. There was no going back to her father – that had just been a little fantasy. That's what Deborah, her father's one-night stand, had really been telling her: be realistic, you might as well forget him.

Anna tried to find out more about Brian and the twins from her mother.

'I wondered if you'd get interested,' her mother said. 'I know you think Brian likes a drink, but you should have seen his ex, the twins' mother. Those boys are doing very well, considering. I feel sorry for her, she's got a problem, but Diarmid and Declan were only seven when I first set eyes on them. Nervous little things, didn't know what day it was.'

'What did she do?'

'I'll spare you the details, but she was vicious. At least she was sometimes, other times she was all over them. They didn't know if they were coming or going.'

She gave Anna a sharp look.

'You aren't the only one with problems.'

'Tell me about it.'

'There you go, you see? All I can say is, if you want to chat about anything, here I am. I haven't been round the world and got university degrees like Wolf's mother but maybe I know more than I let on.'

She couldn't keep an edge out of her voice, and Anna felt a pang of remorse for all the time she'd spent up at Colette's.

'Thanks, Mum.'

They hugged and didn't say any more.

Anna found herself paying more attention to the twins, watching out for them at school as much as anything so she could get to know which was Diarmid, which Declan. She wouldn't be caught out again. And they were different, she discovered, in what they did.

Declan was part of a group of little Whinnies who seemed to spend most of their spare time chubbing – getting wood and old furniture together for the bonfire on Guy Fawkes night. Yes, Whin's other big night of the year was about to happen.

Anna watched them take all evening to drag an old settee up to the top of the field where the mark from last year's bonfire still was.

'It'll be made of that foam stuff,' said Brian. 'It'll smothercate the whole village when they light it.'

He and Diarmid were watching from the same window.

'Why?' asked Diarmid.

'Poly-something-or-other, it gives off fumes. Deadly.'

'Whose d'you think it was, the settee?' asked Anna.

'Well, it's not ours – it's too good. In fact, can we swap it? Cath!' Brian shouted.

'Brian!' Anna hissed.

'Only kidding, pet.'

'It'll be the Phillipses',' said Diarmid. 'It's horrible!'

'No, we'd have seen them throwing it out,' said Anna.

'And,' said Brian, 'we'd have reported them to the council for it!'

The gang had finally got the settee to the top of the field and they all sat down in it. Like the Cranberries album cover, Brian said. He reckoned to keep up with modern Irish music as well as traditional.

'Perhaps if there's plenty of ventilation it'll be all right,' said Brian.

'What do you mean, "if"? It's in a field!' said Anna.

'No flies on you, pet. You'll go far.'

And they laughed together.

It was a wonder Brian could joke about the council. The letters were still coming. Not about the Chevrolet now, that was finally fixed and was totally legal, so Brian said, and it wouldn't be long before he'd be taking them out in it, the whole clan, and Anna could bring along her young fellow for the ride.

No, the letters were still about using the house for hairdressing. They were threatened with eviction if '7 Windermere Grove continued to be used as commercial premises'. The victory of The Bold Fenian Men (and Anna) had been temporary; running battles with the council had become a way of life.

'I'm going to have to get a shop,' said Anna's mother holding up the latest council letter despairingly. 'I can't stand this.'

'They're only trying to scare you off,' said Brian. 'Tell them where to get off.'

'Thank you, Brian, very useful.'

'Well, I ask you – "commercial premises" indeed! They make it sound like a bloody great widgit factory; it's only Jimmy Tat's mother having a perm.'

'What's widgits?' asked Declan.

'And it saves her having to go off to a proper hairdresser's – sorry, Cath, you know what I mean – so she doesn't have to travel out of the village.'

'What's widgits?'

'In fact,' said Brian, warming to his idea, 'social

services should pay you; if this isn't a social service, I don't know what is.'

'What's widgits?'

'Widgits? What're you talking about? There's no such bloody thing!'

Meanwhile Wolf kept low, waiting for the police to decide. He missed the start of the college course.

'They'll give me hell, the other students,' he said gloomily. 'I can't go.'

'Tell them where to get off. And you can't just sit around here all day, it's like being in prison.'

She immediately wished she hadn't said it. Those had been his own words the first time she'd seen him in his room.

'At least we'd have something new to talk about if you were at college,' she said. 'Come on, let's watch "Casualty".'

31

On Friday morning at break the geek came over to her.

'Oh, hi, Aaron. What is it?'

He gave her a folded piece of paper. It was an e-mail. She'd completely forgotten about all that.

'Check your mail regular,' said Aaron. 'There could be something important. Like this.'

From: canislupus<wolfswhinworld@hotmail.com>

To: bananna<bananna@hotmail@hotmail.com>
Subject: freedom!
Date: 28 September 2001 9.32

The case has been dropped – the police aren't going to prosecute! The letter just came this morning and I remembered you can get your mail at school so I had to tell you the good news. Ring me tonight.

The wolf is free!

'Brilliant!' yelled Anna.

Aaron was watching her.

'Thanks, Aaron,' said Anna: 'But I can open my mail myself.'

Though of course she'd completely forgotten she had such a thing as an e-mail address.

'Yeah, I suppose. But you haven't checked it since we started back this term,' he said accusingly. 'You were keen enough to get me to set it up for you.'

Anna shrugged and started to walk away. She didn't need to bother with Aaron any more.

'Interesting mail,' he said.

She turned and looked at him, really looked at him, but she couldn't tell what he was thinking. He blinked behind his glasses.

'I suppose you've read it,' she said accusingly.

'It's only down to me you got it at all,' he said. That meant 'yes'.

'Just keep your beak out!' Anna said.

'Right. It looks like there's a lot to keep out of,' said Aaron. He took off his Harry Potters, rubbed his eyes, then squinted at her. Too much staring at the monitor, thought Anna. In the old films this was when they'd say: 'But you're beautiful!'

God, he was ugly.

'Yeah, there's a lot. Not just wolfswhinworld either. There's other websites. Steffi Fleischman's got one too.'

The name was a cold hand on Anna's heart. How did he know this stuff? Maybe he could hack into any computer system he wanted. Squinty-eyed nerd.

'Who? What you talking about, Aaron?' She tried to keep the panic out of her voice.

Aaron put his glasses back on, shrugged. He obviously thought he had some hold over her.

'Well, if you don't know, happen you should, Anna. Come on, I'll show you,' he said.

But of course he knew she knew, and if he was going to first-name Anna when anybody could have heard, well, it was all getting too creepy. Time to turn him off.

'I'm busy right now. And I don't think the school will be too pleased if they find out number 17 computer's being used for private e-mail.'

'Yeah. But I reckon *aaronsrod* can soon disappear. Leaving *bananna* to cop for it. Let's face it; you haven't got a clue. Anna.'

She stared at him as hard as she'd stared at Diarmid in her bedroom: more going on in there than she'd thought. He turned and walked off down the corridor.

Over the next few days she saw him talking to other schoolkids, looking her way. She didn't trust him.

That night, a very cheerful Wolf on the phone.

'Finished!' He whooped with glee. 'On the run no more, no secrets!'

'Brilliant! Do they say why?'

'The letter doesn't say much, hang on . . .' A rustle of paper. 'It says "charges are not being preferred owning to the non-compliance of the main witness". Colette says it sounds as though Steffi's parents have decided it's not worth it, or maybe Steffi got it wrong all along.'

'Well, good old Steffi.'

'A little touch of sarcasm there, Anna?'

'There might be.'

'Thanks a lot.'

'But what do I know about it? It just means we can all get on with our lives now. So, it's definite then, that's it?' asked Anna again.

'That's what it says here.'

'And, Wolf, college on Monday I hope?'

'Yeah, no reason not to now.'

'You've already missed a month of drawing women with no clothes on – what they do down there I hear. Lucky Wolf.'

He laughed half-heartedly.

'Got to go, Wolf. See you later?'

'Yeah.'

'Brilliant news. See you.'

But Wolf wasn't quite clear of his past yet, and Anna wasn't long in finding out how.

'What's this I'm hearing then, Anna? About your young man?' Lydia asked as soon as Anna walked into the kitchen of The Bull the following day.

'Sorry, Lydia? What are you hearing?'

'In trouble with the police.' She paused expectantly. 'I hear.'

'Don't know what you're on about.' Tell Lydia nothing. And she could hardly say, 'He's not, he's been cleared,' without saying what he'd been cleared of. Who'd Lydia been talking to? Mother of the geek? Someone who'd spotted the police up at Sneck Cottage?

'Been down to Boltby Police Station more than once, I hear.'

'News to me, Lydia.'

'Oh, perhaps he doesn't tell you everything, then. Perhaps he's one of those.'

She was holding two chickens by their feet, one in each hand. She stared at Anna intently. She hadn't finished.

'You want to know why the police are interested in him?'

Anna shrugged, but her heart was pounding.

'Because of what *he's* interested in. Know what that is?'

'I'm sure you'll tell me, Lydia.'

'Young girls, that's what.'

'Don't be stupid.'

'Young girls younger than you.'

'Don't be stupid.'

'You know how young I heard? Eight.'

'Lydia, that is really, really stupid. And you believed who told you? Who was it? Who was it?'

Anna willed her fear into anger.

'Who was it, Lydia? I'll kill them,' Anna screamed.

'Don't get so upset, Anna. I only thought you ought to know seeing as how he's interested in you.'

'Shut your fat, stupid mouth, Lydia. What do you care about me anyway?'

'Ooooh! Temper, temper.'

But anger was the only way Anna could get through. Ten minutes later she was running up to Sneck Cottage, sacked from The Bull. She told him what Lydia had said. She told him about Aaron as well, that he seemed to know a lot, that they couldn't trust him.

'You know, Anna, I've been holed up in this room for months, hardly sticking my nose outside in case someone bit it. After I got the letter yesterday morning I could have done cartwheels, I could have some space. Colette said why didn't I take some junk over to the bonfire. So I'm dragging these old chairs across the field and it's a bit grey out there but there's a wind blowing on my face and I'm thinking: it's over, I'm free, I'm out. And now, a day later...' He shrugged. A day of feeling good, that's all he'd had, and then things had started closing in again.

Anna did her best.

'Perhaps she doesn't really know anything and it's just gossip.'

'Sounds like she knows a lot.'

'But she got stuff wrong, Wolf. I mean, eight!'

'Oh yeah, that's crazy. But what do I do about it? Put an ad in the paper, to correct the record?'

'Perhaps it's only Lydia.'

'Thanks for trying, Anna, but you know as well as me; if Lydia knows, the whole village knows.'

And if Anna needed confirmation of that, Rachel soon provided it, Rachel who hadn't spoken to Anna for weeks. She was sitting on the wall just down from Sneck Cottage. She was waiting for Anna.

'Hi, Anna. Long time no see.'

'Hi, Rach. It's a big place, Whin, you just don't bump into folk.'

'You haven't changed, have you? He hasn't taught you any manners, then, the Wolf?'

Anna thought she'd make an effort. The abortion.

'I was sorry about the, er, it must have been a shit time. For Glenn as well.'

Rachel didn't blink. This was a no-go subject.

'What you on about, Anna, what're you trying to say?'

'Oh, nothing.'

'Me and Glenn are fine. We're engaged.'

'Right. Congratulations. Are you old enough?'

'To get engaged, yeah, it's legal.' She paused for effect. 'Unlike some things.'

'Sorry?'

'I said, unlike some things what aren't legal. Child abuse, for instance. I think you know who I'm on about, Anna.'

'I don't think so.'

'Your friend Wolf, that's who. He's a fucking paedophile, isn't he?'

Anna turned and walked away. No point in staying.

'A fucking paedophile,' Rachel shouted after her. 'And I'll tell you what; no way is he staying in this village. No way!'

The day after, her mother said to Anna, quiet and urgent, 'Anna, what's going on? The things I've just heard about Wolf, what's it mean?'

Lydia and Rachel were one thing, but Anna knew she'd have to level with her mother.

She said what she knew.

She did it awkwardly, because she hadn't planned how to do it, and tearfully, because it had been a secret for too long. Worse, it had been a secret she hadn't shared with her mother but had shared with Colette.

When Anna had finished her mother said, 'It's all his

147

version, what you're telling me, isn't it? So the important question is: is he telling the truth?'

'Well, the police aren't doing any more so they must believe him.'

'No, I'm not asking what the police think, Anna. I'm asking about you. Do you believe him? You've seen a lot of him this summer; do you trust him, how he is with you, not just what he says?'

'I think so.'

'Not good enough, Anna. Has he asked to sleep with you?'

'Mum!'

Her mother sighed. 'Anna, what d'you think I was doing at your age, going to church?'

Anna took a breath.

'Actually, I asked him.'

A worried smile crossed her mother's face.

'And he said no. So I do trust him. Yes.'

Her mother stood up and sighed again.

'Well, I'm not happy about it. He seems a nice boy but you could pick someone more, er, straightforward. And you kept it from me.'

'Colette asked me to. I couldn't say anything.'

'Colette? Colette?' her mother said angrily. 'Anna, who's your mother? Eh? It's me you should be talking to. Remember that.'

Anna hung her head and nodded miserably.

'I must get on; I've got a customer coming. All right, Anna, we'll do what we can to help. Tell Brian when he gets in.'

'Mum! What tonight?'

'You'll have to. I imagine he'll have heard something anyway.'

So she had to do it all again for Brian, upstairs so her mother's customer wouldn't hear the row. Except to Anna's amazement there wasn't any row. Brian nodded as she sat on her bed and told a briefer version, without tears this time.

He just said: 'There's no harm in the lad, you can tell. And you say the police aren't prosecuting? Well, if there was the slightest whiff of anything they'd want to nail him to the wall. We're with you, kid. What's your mother say?'

When they went back downstairs Anna's mother said: 'Funny. She didn't turn up, Mrs Greenhalgh, and she's never missed since I started. And I saw her yesterday in the shop, she was just as usual.'

And she looked thoughtful for the rest of the evening.

32

To begin with, things were no different for Wolf or Colette. Anna managed to persuade Wolf to start at college and Colette ran him down on the Monday to sign up but by Wednesday he was ready to quit.

'I think the other students know,' he said.

'Why, what have they said?' Anna asked.

'Nothing, in so many words.'

'"In so many words"? So what did they do, dance it? Figures, I suppose, they are artists after all,' said Anna scornfully.

'You can just tell.'

'Wolf, you are pathetic. How can you tell? Are they ignoring you?'

'There's one or two who are OK – Kelly's friendly.'

'Male Kelly or female Kelly?'

'Female.'

'Fine, just don't tell me any more about her, right? So what else do they do – put salt in your coffee? Hide your PE kit?'

'Don't, Anna.'

'You need it, Wolf, you are truly pathetic. What you're saying is: nobody's said anything, nobody's done anything, and some are quite friendly – and you're the one who started late! Wolf, watch my lips:

you are doing fine. For God's sake, stop talking yourself down.'

And she kissed him, quickly, full on the mouth.

'So, who's this Kelly, then?'

On Thursday Declan came home and said he wanted to change schools. Anna's mother laughed and asked why.

'No one's talking to me,' he said, looking miserable.

'Aren't any of your old school friends in the same class?'

'Yeah. It's them who aren't speaking, so no one else is neither.'

'You're just imagining things, Declan,' said Anna's mother. 'Why wouldn't they be?'

Declan said nothing, then Diarmid said: 'It's something about Wolf, isn't it, Anna?'

'Like what?' Anna played for time.

Diarmid gave her a straight look. 'You know. Is it true what they're saying? He's wanted for child abuse?'

'Diarmid, do you think Anna would be friends with someone like that?' Anna's mother sounded as confident as she could.

'Suppose not,' Diarmid conceded.

'I'm sorry it's not going too good, boys,' said Anna's mother getting her purse. 'Here, get yourselves something from the shop.'

She gave Anna a look that wasn't entirely sympathetic; she was annoyed that the twins were having to suffer as well.

Aaron was behind it, Anna felt sure. He'd helped her

find Wolf, and now he was trying to – what? Drive him out? And there was nothing she could do.

Because Wolf or Colette hardly ever went out in the village they hadn't felt the mood that was brewing. The first time Colette felt it was when she went into The Bull. Occasionally she would take her book, buy a drink and sit in the corner reading.

She was blazing.

'And last night he says to me – this is the landlord Ron, good old Ron, friend to all including some of the biggest arsewipes you could set eyes on – he says to me, "I don't want to cause a scene, but I'm afraid your custom is no longer appreciated here". I was flabbergasted. I said, "I'm afraid your way of talking isn't appreciated either. Are you barring me from The Bull?"'

She had a gulp of red wine. Anna thought she was a bit drunk.

'Well, whether he wanted a scene or not, he got one. I really burnt my bridges; no going back there, Anna.'

Anna hesitated before she asked, 'Did he say why he was barring you?'

And Colette hesitated too before she said with downcast eyes, 'I didn't ask.'

They were all looking down, and Colette's anger had seeped away.

'Sorry, Colette,' said Wolf, without moving.

Then the graffiti started, sometimes painted on the cottage wall, sometimes painted on paper and nailed to the tree. Sometimes it was short, simple two-word stuff, sometimes it was more complicated.

CHILD ABUSERS OUT OF OUR VILLAGE

WOLFS SHOULD BE EXTINCT

WHO THANKS HEAVEN FOR LITTLE GIRLS?
PAEDOS

Whenever new graffiti appeared Colette would get soapy water and scrub it off. Often it took a lot of scrubbing and she would come back in with her hands red and raw. Anna helped.

Once Colette heard talking outside and went out. There was a group of people painting slogans on the gable end of the cottage. They swore at her before they strolled off laughing.

'They weren't kids. And I don't think they were from Whin,' she told Anna, hardly able to keep the disgust out of her voice as she said the name of the village. Colette rang the police who said they couldn't do anything unless they caught the people responsible actually doing it. A patrol car came and parked on the road for a couple of nights, then stopped coming. The council said it was nothing to do with them as it wasn't council property.

With the days getting shorter there was more darkness to hide what people did. One morning Colette got up to see a wolf hanging by its neck from the tree in the field.

'Of course when I got close,' she told Anna, 'I saw it wasn't a wolf – how could it be? – but an Alsatian. But it's horrible when you think about it – somebody's bothered to get a dead Alsatian, God knows where from, stinking, in their car, to string it up in front of our house.

Think of all that effort! I cut it down before Wolf saw it and dragged it up to the ditch. I suppose it'll rot pretty quickly. Go and have a look if you want.'

'It's OK, Colette, I'll pass on that,' said Anna.

'Anna, how long can they keep doing it for?' There were tears glinting in Colette's eyes.

'Oh, they'll get fed up soon, they're bound to.' But Anna wasn't as confident as she tried to sound.

33

It wasn't just Sneck Cottage that was targeted.

Others besides Mrs Greenhalgh stopped coming to Windermere Grove to have their hair done. Some rang with excuses, some just didn't turn up. The only explanation could be Anna's friendship with Wolf. Her mother said nothing but cheerfully dealt with the ones that kept coming, her chat a bit over-eager.

At school Anna saw Rachel whispering to Aaron. Anna told herself she didn't care and tried to mean it.

But however much Anna was able to stop her own feelings being hurt, she couldn't ignore what was happening in the village. Even Brian seemed less confident about how to fight back when he told them about a petition that had gone up in The Bull demanding that Wolf be removed from the village.

'They're eejits, all of them. I said: "Who's meant to do this removing? The lad's done nothing illegal." They said: "We don't care who does it; we'll do it if we have to." I said: "Jesus, it'll be lynchings next, it'll be like the blacks strung up in Alabama." There's no talking to them, they've all gone mad.'

'Had many signed it?' asked Anna's mother.

'Not many, and I know there's others like me who won't. But there's too many worked themselves up over it. Even Dave, you know, who came to the barbecue, one of me best mates for God's sake, he thinks there might be more to Wolf than meets the eye. They want to believe it. It's crazy.'

Now wasn't the time for Anna to tell Brian that perhaps Dave wasn't one of his best friends.

Declan came home miserable; he'd been thrown out of the chubbing gang. They said they didn't want friends of Wolf's around.

'I said I wasn't,' he said.

'Gee, thanks,' said Anna.

'I don't mean that, it's just he's your friend, Anna. I don't know him, not really.'

'You want an introduction?' asked Anna.

'You're well out of it,' said Diarmid. 'Collecting all that wood and stuff, looks like hard work to me.'

'Oh yeah? You'll all be up there on Saturday,' said Declan.

'Not me, the way things are,' said Anna. 'They can all chuck themselves on the bonfire for me. Good riddance!'

But the next night Declan seemed to be back in with the little Whinnies and even persuaded Anna's mother to part with an old chair that was really too good to be burnt.

'We need something for the top, for the guy to sit on.'

'OK. I suppose it's ready to be thrown out.'

Anna thought Declan was buying his way back into favour with the gang. She eyed Declan suspiciously.

'So how come you're mates again, Declan? What was the deal?'

'What you talking about?' said Declan defensively.

'Get us a chair for the guy, was it? Or sign in blood to say you're definitely, *definitely* not a friend of Wolf?'

'Don't be stupid, Anna.'

'And you're nothing to do with me either, I suppose.'

But there was no point in pushing it. How's a kid meant to keep his friends? The little rat.

Anna and her mother watched Declan carry the chair out to the three kids who were standing waiting round the Chevrolet; they gave a little cheer and grinned. One of them gave the house the finger.

'Are we going up to the bonfire, Anna?' asked her mother.

'No way, not me.'

'It'll be dark, it'll be all right.'

'So what? Wolf's not going to be there, is he? Or Colette? So I'm not, either. You can all suit yourself,' Anna said, knowing full well her mother wouldn't betray her.

'Of course I won't, we won't,' said her mother. 'I just thought it might be a way of, I don't know, building some bridges.'

'Burning them, more like; they'll be on that bonfire already.'

'They're not all part of this stupid campaign thing, you know. Some of my customers have come back already, said things like they were ill. They don't all want this petition; there are some decent people in Whin, Anna.'

'They must be the ones in the church graveyard.'

Her mother sighed. 'See how you feel on Saturday.'

'I know how I'll feel on Saturday.'

34

And when it came round, she didn't feel any different. She went up to see Wolf in the afternoon. He was in the middle of some clay sculpture project.

'I want to finish this and it'll take hours yet.'

'So what is it?'

'A relief.'

'Yeah, we need some of that.'

'A "relief" is a sort of flat sculpture,' he explained.

'I know what a relief is, Wolf. I was making a joke, you know? Lighten the atmosphere a bit.'

She watched him work the clay with a wooden spatula. It was a face. It somehow looked at you and beyond you at the same time. But with the damp clay it had a dull, flat look.

'So who's it meant to be?' she asked.

Wolf said nothing, just looked at her.

'You're joking! You're saying that's me – that slaphead!'

'It'll be all right when it's fired. I hope.' He grimaced.

'It better had be, or you can give it to someone else. Mentioning no names. So you're not up for a movie?'

'Sorry, Anna. Stay and chat if you want, but I'm really into this. College work is the only thing that's keeping me going,' he said.

'Thanks a bunch.'

'Come on, Anna, I'm not counting you.' He looked wounded. 'You're off the scale.'

'Top end, I hope. So on a Saturday night, you're doing homework and I'll be watching TV at home. Great!'

Declan vanished mid-afternoon so he wouldn't have to say where he was going.

It felt odd, the four of them sitting there, ignoring the fact that the second of the year's big village events was going on right then. Diarmid went to the front window.

'I think they're getting it lit,' he said.

'Oh,' said Anna's mother. 'Nice.'

From the kitchen window you could see rockets going up further down the valley, and you could hear distant *whams* seconds after the rockets exploded their showers of sparks. Brian explained to Diarmid that light travelled faster than sound; Anna thought Diarmid did pretty well to take a science lesson instead of going to the bonfire, for something that wasn't his fault.

And she could see, when she allowed herself to glance up the hill that there was some action up at the village bonfire, the first flames licking up through what Declan and his friends had painstakingly built. Black figures stood around, the red faces too far away to recognise.

TV was awful. Diarmid laughed at 'You've Been Framed' while Brian and Anna tried to spoil it for him by saying how it was all set up.

'It's obvious,' said Brian. 'It's all rehearsed.

Someone's told them to carry a tray of drinks and then trip over and fall in the pond, so they can get it on video.'

'Brian, it's only harmless fun,' said Anna's mother.

'I mean, why else would you be filming your da carrying a tray in the garden?'

'Brian!'

Then they channel-hopped from some quiz thing, to the news, to the lottery, back to...

Declan came crashing in through the front door.

'Dad! You'd better come.'

Anna was on her feet. 'What? What's going on?'

'They're planning something.'

'Who?'

'Glenn and his mates. They're acting stupid.'

Brian grabbed the car keys from the kitchen.

'Come on!'

They piled out of the front door and into the car; no need for *We're on our way* this time, and no engine dying on them ten seconds later. They raced up the road to just below Sneck Cottage, where the gate opened into the field.

There was no need to ask what was being planned. The cottage wasn't that far from the now blazing bonfire; a strong, sixteen-year-old could easily lob a burning brand that distance.

Diarmid dived out of the car to open the gate and Anna ran into the cottage. Colette spun round as Anna ran into the kitchen. She said in a voice like stone: 'They won't beat us, Anna.'

Wolf was sitting at the table, his mouth tight and bitter. Then something crashed through an upstairs window.

'Come on!' yelled Anna. Out they went, to face whatever was happening.

The scene would stay with Anna for the rest of her life, awake and in her dreams, sometimes coloured differently, sometimes slow motion, but the same events:

Glenn and his friends, five or six of them and obviously drunk, throwing burning brands at the cottage; the brands roaring as they hurtled through the air, some going out before they hit the walls of the cottage or the outhouse, some not.

The other villagers backing away to the far side of the bonfire, huddling in hypnotised silence.

The Chevrolet circling the bonfire and driving at the stick throwers, horn blaring all the time, making them run off, but not before a stick, still burning, had crashed through an upstairs window, flames flickering inside.

The car coming to a halt just up the field from the bonfire; Anna's mother and Declan getting out and watching Brian as he strode after the scattering stick throwers shouting at them: 'Murdering bastards!'

Brian turning at Declan's shout and everybody watching as the pink Chevrolet slowly rolled backwards, coming to a halt against the settee at the heart of the blazing bonfire; the brief, eternal pause before the petrol tank exploded, as hilariously awful as anything 'You've Been Framed' could do; the effigy of

Wolf in its chair, mobile phone to its ear, burning until its head lolled over and fell off.

The outhouse black and stark against the cottage, now fully ablaze.

It was over an hour before the fire brigade managed to make its way up to the top of the track by which time the roof of the cottage had collapsed in with a great crash of sparks that sailed high over the moors. And when they finally got a hosepipe going it seemed to Anna that it was as pathetic as the Phillipses' piddling boy.

The burnt-out Chevrolet had become a mysterious object of great beauty, the metal glimmering blue and purple in the heat. Everyone stood and watched, their gaze going from the burnt-out car to the burning cottage.

Brian was talking with some of the other villagers, as friendly as if they were in The Bull together. Anna even heard him laugh. It was a strange night; Anna felt everyone had been transformed somehow, but when they talked, all they could say were normal, silly things.

Not Colette though, she said nothing until Anna and her mother persuaded her to come down to their house when she said: 'Is that it? Have they got what they want now?'

Then she and Wolf went down the hill with Anna and her mother and the twins, leaving Brian sharing a can of beer with his best friend Dave. Friendship was a complicated thing, obviously.

35

Colette left the village that night, but this time, unlike after the May Day Dance, she didn't take Wolf. For the rest of Bonfire Night, what was left of it, he slept on the settee at Anna's.

In the morning nobody in the house said much, but they found themselves looking up the field to the two smouldering piles; the remains of the bonfire with the burnt-out car in it, and the collapsed cottage but with the outhouse intact.

It was a grey morning and a fine drizzle drifted down.

Anna stood at the window, holding Wolf's hand, looking up the field. She didn't want to speak. She was sadder than she had ever been in her life before, and completely exhausted with it all.

Later she and Wolf walked up to the cottage and looked into the steaming, smoking mess of it. The firemen were still there, finishing off. Anna felt sick, looking at things she knew well, like the kitchen table she'd sat at with Colette all summer, now scorched and rained on. The indignity of it!

Then Wolf saw the clay sculpture he'd been working on, only a day ago, lying in the debris on the kitchen floor. He made to go and get it.

'Hey, lad!' shouted one of the firemen: 'Keep out of there. It's not safe.'

But Wolf didn't stop, just ran in and grabbed it. He put it down quickly on the grass next to Anna.

'It's still hot!' he grinned.

The fireman came over.

'I thought I told you to keep out, lad,' he said.

Wolf looked him straight in the eye.

'It's my home they've burned; mine. And this is my sculpture. I'm taking it.'

The night had changed Wolf. He was so determined the fireman softened a bit.

'It were only for your own good. It's not safe in there.'

'This is all I want,' said Wolf.

All three of them looked down at the sculpture. The heat had fired the face. Dense colours had been fixed into it, as though it had been pulled out of a volcano. Anna thought if pain had a colour, it would look like that. But did it look like her? Other people would have to decide that.

Using his T-shirt like oven gloves, Wolf carried it back down to Anna's.

Anna's mother said Wolf could stay as long as he wanted; they'd make up a bed in the twins' room for him.

He said: 'Thanks. We'll be staying in Whin. It'll be all right now.'

Overnight he had become sure of who he was and what he wanted. So when later he spoke to Colette, who'd gone to stay with a friend in Leeds, it wasn't a long conversation.

'She's agreed that she'll come back to the village,' he announced. 'She says the insurance will pay for the damage.'

*

164

Wolf was right about the mood in Whin. Something had happened that night. Whatever the mood was that had got hold of everyone, it had suddenly lifted, and the witchhunt had ended. A sort of madness, Anna thought, and now it was over.

But why had it ended? Because they'd got what they wanted, in a way? Because they'd realised how stupid it had been and the burnt-out cottage was a reminder, stuck there in front of their noses? Anna didn't know.

But she knew it was over when she saw Rachel on the school bus on the Monday morning. Rachel glanced away, a bit shifty, then looked straight at Anna.

'Hi, Anna.'

And Anna was amazed to hear herself say, as if it had been a normal weekend: 'Hi, Rach.'

'Stupid, weren't it? The bonfire, all that,' said Rachel.

It was the nearest she'd get to saying sorry.

Where they have hurricanes it must be like that, the day after when everybody looks at what's left and then gets on with making it work again.

It was as though something else had done it to them, rather than they'd done it themselves.

The police asked questions about the fire, but it had been dark of course, and nobody could see very clearly, and perhaps it was just sparks from the bonfire that had started it, and so on. Anna thought she could feel the awkward, slightly guilty mood in the village but no one was going to get prosecuted; that was clear.

Glenn didn't escape entirely, though. There was a cottage to rebuild. When the rebuilding started weeks later, by Rachel's father again, the rumour was that he was making Glenn work on Sneck Cottage, without wages.

'If lads act t'goat, they'll have to tek t'consequences,' said Rachel's father.

It was a sort of justice.

The petition was quietly dropped and Ron in The Bull offered Anna her job back. He also made it known to Anna that Colette was welcome to come in again. She could even 'sit there reading her bloody book', as he put it. He even organised a collection to help replace the Chevrolet. The cottage might have been insured but the Chevvy wasn't.

'When Ron handed the money over,' Brian reported, 'I couldn't help it, I was in tears. That's what mates are for. You know what he said? "Only one condition, Brian; you buy something on wheels, not bricks!" Anyway, gang, we're going to have to learn a new song; I've seen the car we want, a Mustang. She's a belter. Have yous heard of a song called "Mustang Sally"?'

Wolf took his sculpture into college; it got top marks.

'My lecturer wants to buy it,' he laughed. 'I told her it's not for sale, it's an unrepeatable process.'

'And did Kelly like it?' asked Anna.

'I don't think she understood it.'

'I'm sure you can explain it to her.'

Wolf laughed ambiguously.

Ah, Wolf, what happened to the timid boy who couldn't even stand up to his parents? And who's this good-looker who might start to play around? Things were moving on.

Anna's dad rang.

'*Hiya, pet!*'

'Hi, Dad!'

'*Any news?*'

Where do I start?

'Brian's getting a new car,' she said.

'*Oh yeah? One that goes?*'

'I doubt it.'

They laughed together.

'*I've got some wheels now; I'm thinking of coming over.*'

Anna groaned.

'*No, angel, straight up.*'

'Let me guess, next Saturday.'

'*That's right. How did you know?*'

'Forget it. Yeah, it'll be great to see you.'

'*Both of us. I'm still with Deborah.*'

'That's great. I think she's got your measure, Dad.'

'*She's struck on you, too, pet. She thinks you're something else.*'

She's right there. Whatever I was six months ago, I'm something else now.

'*Got to run, pet. Say hello to your mother for me, and the O'Blarneys. See you, Anna.*'